WHEELER ANTABANEZ

THE OLD ASYLUM

And Other Stories

Sagging
Meniscus

Printed in the United States of America.
Set in Williams Caslon Text with LaTeX.

ISBN: 978-1-944697-01-3 (paperback)
ISBN: 978-1-944697-02-0 (ebook)
Library of Congress Control Number: 2016934032

Sagging Meniscus Press
web: http://www.saggingmeniscus.com/
email: info@saggingmeniscus.com

Reception at the Old Asylum

"They brought the new patients in through the back at Reception. One night the cops brought a lady completely nude and bleeding from the wrists where the cuffs had cut her. She was raving and fighting, but a doctor in a white coat gave her a shot of something that knocked her out cold. Turns out she had just been arrested for drowning her babies in the bathtub."

—from a patient diary left behind on the wards

These stories are dedicated
to the weirdos who frequented the Old Asylum
and loved it as much as I did
This book is for you

"As children, most of us had paid a visit at some time to that forbidden place, and later we carried with us memories of our somber adventures. Over the years we came to compare what we experienced, compiling this knowledge of the asylum until it became unseemly to augment it further.

By all accounts that old institution was a chamber of horrors, if not in its entirety then at least in certain isolated corners. It was not simply that a particular room attracted notice for its atmosphere of desolation: the gray walls pocked like sponges, the floor filthied by the years entering freely through broken windows, and the shallow bed withered after supporting so many nights of futile tears and screaming. There was something more."

– Thomas Ligotti,
"Dr. Locrian's Asylum,"
Songs of a Dead Dreamer

The

Old

Asylum

Table of Contents

Front Male Hill

"The men were thrown in cells with their pores opened up and the alcohol leaking out of them. They always scream for the first few days and it was hard to listen. After they detoxed, the nurses let them sit on the porch and smoke tobacco from corncob pipes. The staff kept a supply of these inexpensive pipes because the patients' hands were often too shaky to roll their own cigarettes."

—from a 1966 newspaper clipping found in the Administration Building

Behind the Old Asylum

"Last summer, an elderly female went missing from the geriatric ward and they couldn't find her for almost a week. She eventually turned up in the woods behind the asylum where it was surmised that she fell, broke her hip and succumbed to exposure. Animals had partially eaten her body and the birds took her eyes. She had no family to mourn her passing and her remains went unclaimed. She is buried in an unmarked grave at the potter's field."

—*from a patient diary left behind on the wards*

The Old Asylum

re you seriously going to take her up to the Old Asylum? You're crazy. For real, I don't think she can handle it. Angela Jacobs isn't exactly the type of girl who is going to appreciate the finer points of the sanitarium. Although, it might just scare the pants off her, I'll give you that."

Hunter laughed and punched his friend Joey in the arm, "I'm just gonna take her up there and show her around that's all. Besides, she asked me to *guide* her so I don't even know if it's a date or anything. I think she's just curious about the abandoned buildings and stuff."

"Oh she's curious alright," replied Joey. "She's curious about why you broke up with Susan last week, she's curious about that half ounce of sour diesel in your backpack, and I would dare say that she is most definitely curious about that bulge in your pants."

"You're an idiot," Hunter said chuckling, "Stop looking at my bulge, loser. Let's smoke a bowl at your house and then I have to get ready."

Walking the four suburban blocks from Joey's, feeling pleasantly stoned, Hunter got a text from Angela confirming their plans for the night. He shot her back a few smiley faces and bounded up the front steps of his own house. The smell of dinner hung pleasantly in the air and his mother gave him a kiss on the cheek saying, "Wash up for supper."

"Angela Jacobs is stopping by after dinner and we're going to take a walk together."

"Oh?" His mother replied, "Are you sure she doesn't want to come for dinner?"

"No, That's ok. We already made plans for seven."

"Wow, Angela Jacobs huh? That's a nice surprise. She's such a beautiful girl from such a lovely family. Do you want to ask your father to borrow the car?"

"Nah, that's ok. I'm gonna show her around the woods and stuff where we hang out."

"Hunter, I don't want you taking that girl into the abandoned hospital up there. You know I don't like you going in the Old Asylum. It's illegal, it's dangerous, and I certainly don't want you taking Angela Jacobs in there. Her parents would have a conniption fit if they found out. I mean her father is a police officer for goodness sake."

"Relax Mom, we're just going for a nice walk in the woods. It's not a big deal."

"Okay, but you better be telling me the truth. Go say hello to your dad and tell him that dinner will be ready in ten minutes. And I mean it; don't be taking that pretty young woman up to that decrepit old mental hospital. For as long as I live I will never understand your fascination with that horrible place."

After supper Hunter went upstairs and rolled two joints from his bag of weed. He carefully placed them into a plastic baseball card case and snapped it shut. Just as he was slipping the case into his back pocket he heard his mother call upstairs, "Hunter honey Angela Jacobs is here."

Hunter took a quick look in the mirror, ran his fingers through his unruly hair, and hustled down the stairs. In the dining room, his mom was bombarding Angela with a flurry of mundane questions about school. Hunter sought to rescue her from this polite interrogation, but he could tell that Angela was charming his mom and seemed to be at ease with the conversation. When they were finally able to break free and start their walk Hunter said, "Sorry about that. My mom can be pretty nosy at times."

Angela laughed and said, "Are you kidding me? My dad is a detective. I get the third degree every time I come home."

"Oh man, I bet. What did your dad say when you told him you were hanging out with me tonight?"

"Well, I didn't exactly tell him where we're going, but he doesn't mind me hanging out with you. I mean we've gone to school together since kindergarten so my dad sees you as safe. Obviously he doesn't know about your extracurricular activities, but that can be our little secret. Basically, he thinks you're harmless."

"Ha ha, well let's hope he doesn't find out otherwise. Speaking of extracurricular activities…" Hunter pulled the clear case out and flashed her the two joints. "I brought us a little something to enhance the effect of the Old Asylum."

She squealed in delight as Hunter slipped the case back into his pocket and asked him, "Is that still the sour diesel from Adam Nash?"

"Yeah I got a half ounce of it today. I'm pretty sure the rest of the QP will be gone by tonight. The supply is dwindling fast so I grabbed all I could afford."

Approaching the dead end of Hunter's street, the young couple stepped around the metal gate and entered the Old Asylum woods. The trees were just starting their autumnal change and both teenagers instinctively lowered their voices in unconscious reverence for the ancient forest. Angela asked in a hushed tone, "So why did you break up with Susan, if you don't mind me asking?"

"No, it's ok. I don't mind talking about it. I liked Susan a lot and she has lots of really good qualities, but there were a few things I couldn't get past. When we were sophomores it was fun to be with her and we laughed all the time, but by the end of junior year she was always jealous about stupid stuff and we fought constantly. My parents didn't really approve of the relationship anymore and I wanted to start out fresh as a senior. I guess once the summer was over, it was also the end for me and Susan. She doesn't admit it, but the breakup was pretty much mutual."

Angela said, "I heard she's been hanging out with Rob Andulski a lot. That's crazy!"

"Yeah I heard that," Hunter sighed. "She always tried to use him to make me jealous so I pretty much knew that would happen. As long as she's happy I don't care what she does. Honestly, I'm pretty much over it."

"Yeah, but come on, Rob Andulski? You've got to be kidding me. That guy is a freakin caveman psycho. You know how many times my dad has arrested that kid? He is seriously dangerous. We've only been back at school one week and Rob already managed to get himself suspended."

"Are you serious? What for?"

"Oh my gosh I can't believe you didn't hear! He pulled down Alfred Hendrickson's shorts in the middle of gym class today. I was there actually and I saw Al's hairy butt. I can't believe you didn't hear about that." They both began to giggle and their mirth rang out through the forest. When they finally stopped laughing, Angela turned serious again and said to Hunter, "So tell me about the Old Asylum. Everyone at school says you're like the expert on the place."

"Ha ha, well I don't know about being an expert. I lived

on Glenview Road my whole life so I was always playing in these woods. It didn't take us long to find the sanitarium when we were little, so I guess I've been exploring the buildings since I was nine or ten. Last year I went to the county library and researched a project about the Old Asylum for Mrs. Feynman's class. I learned a ton of history and stuff about the place. You wouldn't believe it! A lot of people died up there."

Angela said, "My dad told me stories about the potter's field up on the hill. Supposedly it's just a mass grave where they used to bury the mental patients when they died on the wards."

"Yes that's true," Hunter confirmed. "That section is all the way over on the other side of the property by Sepulcher Hill Cemetery. I usually don't go over there because it's too close to the part of the hospital that's still in operation. Plus, it's spooky as hell."

"What and the Old Asylum isn't?"

"The Old Asylum is definitely spooky there's no doubt about that. I still get chills up my spine whenever I go inside, but there's something about the potter's field that just feels wrong. I don't know, maybe I'm crazy, but truthfully I don't know anyone who hangs out there. Besides it's just an overgrown field with a bunch of rickety old crosses…"

Hunter suddenly stopped in his tracks and cocked his head to listen to the woods around them. Angela followed suit and stood motionless. After a moment of careful listening she whispered, "What is it? What did you hear?"

He was standing rigid, listening for a repetition of the sound. After a few moments he relaxed and said, "Probably nothing. I thought I heard a twig snap. Could have been a deer or something. Let's keep going. We're almost there."

The path had been leading them steadily upward as

they approached the abandoned hospital. The last bit of trail was rocky and steep. Hunter took Angela's hand and guided her to the top. At the summit they continued to hold hands and Angela grinned as she gazed at Hunter's handsome face in the golden sunlight. He smiled back at her and for a moment they became lost in each other's eyes. This silent staring may very well have led to a kiss, but Hunter raised his arm and pointed at the top of the trees where a massive red brick insane asylum loomed in the gathering twilight. He whispered, "There it is."

"Wow it's huge!"

"Yeah and that's just the back entrance to the Front Male Ward. The rest of the hospital sprawls out toward Sepulcher Hill. Wait till you see it! In the basement there are long steam tunnels connecting this building with the rest of the Old Asylum. I usually go up on the roof here and smoke before walking around. You ready?"

Angela looked up at the forbidding six-story building with its broken windows and graffiti-stained facade. She was experiencing second thoughts about actually going inside and asked, "Do you think there's anybody else in there? It's a little scarier than I thought it would be."

"There might be people in there, but I doubt it. Even if there are other trespassers it won't really matter. I've been coming here since I was little and never once had a problem. The view from the roof is amazing. You can see New York City perfectly, especially at night." Hunter gave her hand a reassuring squeeze and said, "Let's go. It will be all right. I've done this a thousand times."

The door to this particular entrance of the Old Asylum had long been torn from its hinges. As the teenagers passed through the anteroom, the air temperature noticeably dropped by several degrees. Angela shivered in the darkness, as much from the cold sanitarium air as from fear, but the crumbling first floor dayroom held no surprises for Hunter. He didn't usually like to use a light in the building because it caused night blindness and attracted unwanted attention, but to make her feel better he flicked on a flashlight and lit the way.

Turning down a hallway lined with padded cells, Hunter started up a running commentary that he hoped would help Angela feel more at ease, "This ward is where the male alcoholics would sweat out the booze when they came to dry out. They used to keep beer here to wean them off liquor. Me and Joey once found a case of Pabst bottles from the 1800s."

"Wow what did you do with them? Were they still any good?"

"Ha ha no such luck. Actually they were empty. We didn't do much with them, just took 'em up on the roof and threw them off, one by one, down into the courtyard. That was a fun day. Another time Joey and I found a half-full jar of morphine in the administration building. It was in a brown bottle with a skull and crossbones on the label. I wanted to keep it, but Joey called dibs and, besides, he saw it first. I'm pretty sure he still has it somewhere, probably under one of the dirty clothes piles in his room."

"That's crazy. You guys didn't try any of it, did you?"

"Nah, first of all, that part of the hospital shut down in the 1970's so the morphine was super old. Second of all, I don't think I would ever try opiates. Weed is a good thing and I have a few beers from time to time, but I'm not really into the idea of becoming a drug addict."

"How are we going to get up on the roof?"

"There's a staircase at the end of this hall and then on the top floor you have to climb up a ladder, but it's not scary or anything. Up on the roof there's a nice sized concrete platform where we can hang out and enjoy the view. From up there you can see the entire Old Asylum complex and, if it's a clear night, we should be able to see the city lights."

As they started up the stairs Angela relinquished Hunter's hand, but kept very close as he led her to the sixth floor. The rusty paint chipped door on the top landing had the words *WELCOME TO HELL* spray-painted in thick black letters above the doorjamb. When Hunter tried to pull it open the door stuck, but on the second hard tug it gave way with a loud creaking groan and a shower of paint flakes.

Sticking his head cautiously around the doorframe, Hunter peered down the sixth floor hallway, listening and smelling for the presence of other trespassers. Sensing the coast was clear, he took Angela's hand once again and led the way. There was more light up here from the setting sun than there had been downstairs, but instead of making Angela feel more secure, the long shadows enhanced the spookiness of the abandoned mental ward. Walking down the vandalized corridor, Angela found that for the first time in her life, she was truly terrified. She had never imagined that a place so scary could actually exist this close to home.

Sensing her heightened fear, Hunter started up his running commentary again and it seemed to soothe her a bit, "Don't worry we're almost there. Joey and I found this way up to the roof like four years ago and I pretty much come up here all the time." As if to prove this fact, Hunter stopped at an unmarked door that looked as if it might be a broom closet. He turned the knob with a creak and opened the door, revealing a slim set of wooden stairs that ascended into the ceiling. "This is the attic. It's full of pigeons and smells terrible, but don't worry, we won't be in there long. The ladder to the roof is just at the top of the stairs."

The steps creaked as Angela followed Hunter into the attic and the acrid smell of bird droppings hung heavy in the stagnant air. It was inky dark except for a shaft of light pouring in through a ladder hatch in the roof. Hunter sent Angela up the steel ladder first and then followed close behind. As she poked her head out of the hatch, Angela exclaimed, "Oh my gosh, this is amazing Hunter. The view from up here is incredible and this breeze feels so good. I was wondering how you could hang out in such a ridiculously horrible place, but coming up here and seeing this, I think I'm starting to understand."

Taking her hand again, Hunter led Angela over to middle of the observation deck where two plastic hospital chairs were conveniently positioned to face the sunset. Hunter used his bare hand to wipe some of the dust off the seats and they both sat down with smiles on their faces. Producing the joint case, Hunter wasted no time lighting one up. There was an easy, contented quiet between them as they passed the well-rolled joint and watched the sun going down behind the western edge of the woods. Angela spoke first, saying quietly, "It was scary as hell getting up here, but this is such a romantic spot. I wouldn't want to be here with anybody but you Hunt."

Hunter blushed a bit, but the dwindling light masked the color on his cheeks. He thought to himself, *I should kiss her now*, but instead he raised his arm and pointed to a well-lit area on the other side of the campus. "See the big building with the lights on? That's the section of hospital still in operation. There are inmates in there right now on the wards. The county is building a new psychiatric facility down the hill and it won't be long before the patients get transferred. I can't wait to explore that building. That's where the morgue supposedly is, but I haven't seen it yet. They have this recreation cage with razor wire on the top where the inmates go to smoke cigarettes. Sometimes we creep up and watch them from the woods. They're freaky looking, especially the way they shuffle around outside in their slippers. They wear hospital gowns and their eyes are drugged up like zombies."

Angela squirmed in her seat and begged, "Please don't talk about mental patient zombies. Not while we're up here. I was just starting to not be scared anymore. Tell me a happy story about the Old Asylum."

"Hmmmmm," Hunter thought hard about the history he had learned and tried to think of a single happy story about the abandoned mental hospital. "To tell you the truth, there aren't many happy stories about this place. The people locked away in those padded cells downstairs were there for a good reason and I'm pretty sure they weren't very happy about it. I read in the library that back in the 1930's, during a really bad winter, the boilers exploded and the entire hospital lost heat. They weren't able to fix the problem for over two weeks. In the meantime, twenty four patients actually froze to death in their cells. It caused a huge scandal in the community and the hospital administration was accused of neglect. I think some of them were fired because of it. The worst part was the ground was frozen and they couldn't dig graves for the bodies until springtime. They had to keep all the corpses in the cafeteria freezers and apparently the entire hospital reeked of decaying flesh."

Angela looked at Hunter aghast and said, "That is the worst happy story I have ever heard! What the hell,

Hunter! I ask you to tell me a happy story and you go on about all the people who have died here. Jeeez!"

"Ha Ha. Sorry. Actually those twenty four inmates were just a small portion of the patients who lost their lives here, but…"

"HUNTER!" Angela broke in laughing, "You better tell me a happy story right now or I'll never forgive you."

Hunter smiled and snuffed out the small nub of the roach against the bottom of his sneaker. He asked her, "How are you feeling? Wanna smoke the other joint? I'm not as stoned as I could be."

"Yes I do, but don't change the subject. Tell me something pleasant about our surroundings before I start to freak out."

Hunter lit the second joint, took a few deep puffs, and passed it over to Angela. "Let's see, let's see, happy story, happy story. Okay, here's a happy story about the Old Asylum. One day the prettiest girl in school came up to me and asked if I would accompany her to the Old Asylum. She heard some spooky stories about the abandoned hospital and wanted to see it for herself."

Angela squealed with pleasure and passed the joint. She said, "OOOH, I like *this* story. Keep going!"

"Okay, well, this girl, who as I said is the prettiest girl in school, asked me to go up to the Old Asylum with her. Of course I agreed. There was never any question about that. She met me at my house and we walked up through the woods. I held her hand along the steepest part of the trail and when we got to the top, we stared into each other's eyes. Inside the sanitarium she was a little nervous, but she looked extremely cute as she summoned her courage and followed me upstairs to the roof. Once on the observation deck, we sat for a long time smoking weed, talking and laughing. I didn't know how to tell her exactly at the time, but it was one of the happiest nights of my life."

Angela was almost breathless as she said, "I love that story Hunter and I love the way you tell it, but how does it end?"

"Well, the prettiest girl in school and I sat there on the roof talking and smoking for a long time. We watched the sun go down and had an awesome conversation. She asked me to tell her stories and I did my best, but when I finally ran out of things to say, I closed my eyes and kissed her."

The moon had risen over the Old Asylum, casting its blue light across the faces of the teenagers seated on the roof. The night was intensely beautiful and the city twinkled behind them, but the couple was no longer concerned about scenery. Angela's green eyes shimmered. As she began to close them, Hunter leaned in and kissed her. When their lips touched for the first time, a bolt of energy shot through their bodies and soon they were in each other's arms. The first long kiss turned into a series of even longer kisses. The joint between Hunter's fingers burned out and was forgotten.

Angela was the first to break the contact. She giggled and whispered, "Ooooh that was a happy story. Thank you Hunter. I can't wait for the next one."

Hunter leaned in and kissed her again. The moon continued to rise. A great horned owl hooted as it flew past the teenagers, high atop the Old Asylum.

A Warning or an Invitation?

"Entering the wards after they were abandoned was against the law. Even walking on the hospital grounds could be cause for arrest if a cop car rolled up. Despite the consequences, some of us were irrepressibly drawn to the abandoned sections of the mental hospital. It was during these covert visits that the patient relics were uncovered and documented. Moldy diaries, hospital records, and personal letters rose to the surface as we shuffled through the trash. Reading through the discarded papers, we began to get a sense of the agony the inmates of the Old Asylum were forced to endure."

—from the author's private notebook

Reception Looms

"There was a man on my ward with a habit of eating bugs. This place is filthy with insects so there was no shortage of food for him. He was an old man who posed no threat and was allowed to leave the floor for short walks around the hospital. On one occasion someone must have left the door to the roof unlocked because he jumped off and was killed. Nobody missed him much, but since he died there has been an overabundance of cockroaches and millipedes. I guess he was really making a dent in the population."

—from an unfinished letter dated 1977 found in a desk of the Reception building

The Boy Who Loved Halloween

School was out for the day, the trees were golden yellow, and the fall sunshine was at its finest. As Charlie's bicycle steadily gained momentum, the headwinds whipped his long blonde hair from the Halloween mask strapped across his face. The afternoon was unseasonably warm, but Charlie found himself thinking about the upcoming winter when he would have to stow his bike in the shed and start carpooling again. "Only happy thoughts today," he mumbled under his mask. "Only happy thoughts on Halloween."

Every year, starting on the first of November, when it was generally too cold for bike riding, Charlie's parents paid for him to ride back and forth to school in Mrs. Anderson's green station wagon. This left him stuck in the car all winter with his three most hated enemies. The first was Eddy Anderson, a tall, meaty kid with fat bulging cheeks who always smelled faintly of sweat and liked to give Charlie a dead arm every chance he got. The other two were the Everly twins, Michael and Michelle, who lived two houses down from the Andersons. Both twins were beautiful children and considered to be the most popular students in the seventh grade. They had straight blonde hair, blue eyes and sported identical dimples on their cheeks that seemed to melt everyone around them. They also had a cruel streak and, to Charlie, the twins were even more dangerous than Eddy. They never missed an opportunity to make him feel small and always got away with it by flashing their pearly twin smiles.

The worst part about riding in the carpool, and going to school in general, was that none of kids liked Charlie. In fact, they hated him. Even Mrs. Anderson, who received a small payment for driving Charlie to school, didn't care for the boy. When the carpool was first established back in kindergarten, Eddy Anderson had learned that a good way to gain approval from the twins was to pick on Charlie from the safety of the front seat. Eddy wasn't particularly bright in class, but amongst his peers he had a quick tongue and knew how to shape his words into cruel barbs. In the car, Mrs. Anderson wouldn't let Eddy's bullying go too far, but it was obvious that she gained a certain satisfaction from watching her boy make fun of Charlie.

"Only happy thoughts on Halloween!" He repeated to himself and tried to shift his mind in the same way he shifted his bicycle gears. To ease his worrying, Charlie thought back to a guaranteed happy thought: his first awakening to the joy of Halloween. It was a day he remembered with perfect clarity even though he had only been eight years old at the time. The memory held a sweetness like few others for Charlie and it was easy for him to slip back into the Halloween mood as he conjured up the recollection. It was a simple occurrence really, but it had changed his life. He had been accompanying his mother to the grocery store and the Meat Manager who ran the butcher department happened to be entering the shop at the same moment Charlie and his mom were leaving. Right there in front of the gumball machines the Meat Manager stopped in front of Charlie and asked in a loud voice, "HOW YOU DOING LITTLE BUDDY? ARE YOU READY FOR THE BESTEST DARN HOLIDAY IN THE WHOLE WIDE WORLD? HALLOWEEN!"

Normally Charlie would have been shy around an adult, especially one so loud and boisterous, but something about the Meat Manager's authentic excitement for Halloween was infectious. His mother tightened her grip on his hand to reassure him, but to her surprise Charlie was grinning from ear to ear, goggling up at the Meat Manager with a look of wonder in his eyes. After politely asking Charlie's mom if it was okay, the Meat Manager reached into the pocket of his bloodstained apron and pulled out a chocolate peanut butter cup in a sealed wrapper. He slipped the candy into Charlie's hand and clapped him on the back while saying, "Happy Halloween little buddy! Hope you have a great one this year!"

Ever since that moment, Charlie had been bonkers for Halloween. So much so, that dressing up on October 31st just wasn't enough for him. One of the main reasons that nobody at school seemed to care for Charlie was that he wore Halloween costumes every day of the year. It also didn't help that most of his outfits leaned towards the grotesque and some of them were downright scary. He had been warned by the principal numerous times to stop smearing fake blood all over himself before class, he was banned from wearing a mask on school grounds, and he was no longer allowed to talk about vampires, skeletons, or werewolves in classroom discussions. The administration hated Charlie's costume fetish and stood in his way as much as the school charter would allow, but he always found a way to subtly alter his dress in a manner to make it clear that he was in costume.

His parents thought he would eventually grow out of his "dress up stage," but if anything, Charlie's theatrical clothing and props became more elaborate and sophisticated as he got older. He also found new and creative ways to circumvent the ban on masks, such as wearing subtle makeup to make himself look vampiric, or dressing in a tattered black suit in the spirit of a reanimated corpse. This was his thirteenth Halloween and Charlie was quite a sight to behold as he raced his bicycle up the foothills of Mountain Ave. His long cape billowed out behind his black skeleton pajamas and the skull-rack of antlers on his mask bobbed furiously over the handlebars as he stood to pump the pedals. Some motorists invariably slowed down to gawk at the strange skull-faced creature pedaling furiously up the steep incline, but the locals passed by unfazed, well used to the masked boy on his bike.

Charlie had quite a collection of costumes and masks, some of them store bought, but most of them homemade. He had enough masks hanging from hooks on the walls of his room to wear a different face every day of the year without repeating himself. Today he was wearing his latest creation built out of wire mesh and papier-mâché. The deer antlers attached to the cranium of the skull were from the woods behind his house and succeeded in giving the boy a demonic countenance. Since it was Halloween, he had been given special permission to wear the mask all day at school. Many of the children ridiculed him for it, especially when he kept the mask on during lunch, but their insults couldn't touch Charlie behind the safety of his artificial face.

Charlie had been making masks for years and, despite his youth; he had mastered the craft to an advanced degree. As a result of his growing expertise, this particular felt-lined mask was comfortable enough to wear all day, or at least it had been. Presently, as he peddled the flat ground between hills, the mask was getting a bit stuffy and Charlie was working up a sweat. He knew that if he could just make it up this last stretch, he would be able to coast the rest of the way home on a long downhill slope leading right to his driveway. The last steep incline up to the top of Mountain Avenue was his bike riding nemesis, but ever since his thirteenth birthday, he had refused to get off his bike and walk it, no matter how rubbery his legs felt near the top. As he summited the hill for possibly the last time that year, he was greeted with a bird's eye view of the valley and a mile and a half of downhill pavement unfolding before him. It was always this last hill that he looked forward to most.

He allowed himself to pause at the top for a rest and put his foot down on the shoulder of the busy road as the cars flew past. In the valley to his left he could see the suburban houses sprawling across the New Jersey landscape like a crusty scab. To his right, shadows of clouds rolled gently along the contours of Mr. Johnson's farm. The sagging wooden barn and ancient farmhouse were a throwback to a better time, creating a small oasis of preserved agriculture amongst the McMansions and condominiums. To Charlie, Mr. Johnson's fields seemed to go on for miles into the horizon, although in actuality the property was only a few acres of well-tilled land crammed in amongst the sprawl.

Rows of late season Indian corn swayed in the breeze and there was a neat pile of pumpkins stacked in front of the weathered farm stand. Before him was the road: two lanes of black hardtop with a double yellow line leading into the valley. Charlie had his breath back now and without further hesitation jumped on the pedals and let gravity take him. Tears ran from his eyes as the wind entered the holes of his mask and he squinted with cold determination, committing to the steep descent. Fearlessly he raced down the blurred pavement of the mountainous hill, laughing maniacally behind his mask.

Farmer Joe Johnson looked up from his perch high atop his blue tractor and saw Charlie coming fast. As the bicycle closed the distance, the farmer could see the grinning skull mask gleaming in the sun and Charlie's golden hair blowing wild in the wind. The boy's back was arched along the frame of the bike and his black cape whipped around his shoulders like a set of wings. Mr. Johnson smiled and killed the tractor's engine, waving to Charlie and signaling him to pull over by the roadside stand.

One hundred yards away, Charlie saw the farmer and was confronted with a paradox of emotions that made him feel happy, but also clouded the joy he was feeling on the hill. Although Charlie enjoyed Mr. Johnson's company and respected the man, he was by no means eager to stop for a chat. The torment and the agony that social situations brought up inside Charlie were often too much to handle. In his mind, even the most trivial conversations would be picked apart and analyzed, so he tended to avoid talking to people whenever possible. Although Charlie liked the simple farmer, he found himself wishing he could feel the freedom of his bicycle forever, without ever running out of hill or touching the brakes again.

Charlie's feet returned to the earth by the side of the road next to Mr. Johnson's tractor. "How do Charlie?" Said the farmer with a grin. "Did they let you wear a mask at school today seeing as it's Halloween?"

Charlie replied, "Yes! Incredibly, they let me keep it

on all day. I can't believe I managed to get away with it."

The farmer laughed out loud and said, "This is the one day of the year when you can actually be yourself, huh kiddo?" Charlie smiled under his mask and although Farmer Johnston couldn't see it, he sensed it. "Looks like you might need some air in that back tire pal. It's looking a little flat."

Charlie's voice was muffled by the mask as he replied, "I know, I'm gonna pump it up when I get home."

"Good idea. The way you ride that bike it needs to be in top working order or else you're gonna hit the pavement."

"I know," said Charlie with a smile. "I like to go fast."

"Nothing wrong with that boy. Maybe you should try wearing a helmet though. That mask is pretty cool, but a helmet could save your life someday."

"O.K. Mr. Johnson."

"Dammit boy! Enough with that Mr. Johnson act! I told you to call me Joe three years ago and you still won't do it."

"Sorry Mr. Johnson."

The farmer tipped his head back and laughed, his big cheeks sucking in air and making Charlie feel at ease. Charlie had always liked this farmer and it was times like this that he remembered why. Mr. Johnson did not require anything at all from him and was probably the only person who got a kick out of his strange and sometimes awkward dress up games.

"You better get going Charlie. You don't want to miss out on trick or treating. Tell your Mom and Dad I said Hello."

"Will do Mr…. Joe," said Charlie. "Happy Halloween Joe! I'll see you later."

And with that he was back on the road peddling fast with the traffic, trying to catch up on some of the speed he had lost.

Just as he was almost out of earshot Farmer Johnson yelled after Charlie, "BE CAREFUL ON THE ROAD BOY!"

Charlie was just getting up to speed when he heard Mr. Johnson yell something behind him. He was concentrating on pedaling, but didn't want to seem impolite, so turned around to look over his shoulder.

The farmer saw Charlie turn his head, the grotesque demon face appearing hideous as it leered back at him. Instantly Mr. Johnson regretted calling to Charlie because as the boy turned around, the bike wobbled and swerved into the busy road. There was a moment of horror when the farmer saw what would happen and his heart skipped a beat. Helplessly he watched as Charlie veered into the path of a green station wagon barreling down the hill. Then there was the heartbreaking impact and the accompanying screech of tires as the station wagon clipped Charlie's back wheel and spilled him onto the asphalt. The car bucked as it ran over Charlie and the bike, both of which became lodged beneath the undercarriage and were dragged for thirty feet as the station wagon came to a smoking, screeching halt.

Mrs. Anderson sat behind the steering wheel in a state of silent shock. Eddy Anderson had bitten his tongue and was hysterically crying in the passenger seat. The Everly twins screamed in the back. Charlie's mutilated body lay under the car.

As the farmer ran down the shoulder of the road to the accident site, he could see a trail of blood leading under the back bumper. When he got to the car, Farmer Johnson reached into the driver's side window, turned the ignition switch off, removed the keys and threw them onto the dashboard with a flick of his wrist. Once the vehicle was secure, he dropped to his hands and knees and looked under the station wagon.

There was Charlie, crumpled under the chassis like a piece of common road kill. It was obvious to the farmer that he was dead from the position of his body, but he wanted to see the boy's eyes to be sure. The skull mask strapped to Charlie's face was still grinning, this time through a patina of blood that was all too real. Farmer Johnson reached out to pull the mask off, but as he looked closer, he could see that one of the antlers had been pushed through the forehead of the mask and was now buried deep inside Charlie's brainpan. Removing the mask would be a job for the medical examiner.

Feeling disgusted and distraught, the Farmer struggled to his feet and staggered away from the car. Suddenly he felt wretchedly sick and although he hadn't vomited in over a decade, he lost his lunch on the side of the road. All traffic on Mountain Ave had ceased and it wasn't long before several police cars were on the scene. The cops sought to question the occupants of the vehicle, but Mrs. Anderson and the three children were unable to answer with anything but screams.

As the farmer was wiping the last of the vomit from his mouth, a motorcycle cop pulled up next to him on the shoulder of the road, clicked down the kickstand of his bike and killed the engine of his Harley. The cop had known the farmer for many years so addressed him by name, "What in the name of holy heck happened here Joseph?"

The farmer felt another wave of nausea as he said, "It was my fault. I yelled for him to be careful on his bicycle.

He turned around to look at me and accidentally swerved into traffic. He turned around when I called him and then got hit by a car. He's dead. He's under that station wagon and he's dead."

Another patrolmen who had been examining the scene looked under the car and said, "What the hell is wrong with his face? It looks like all the skin was scraped off and the skull is exposed."

Farmer Joe overheard the comment and yelled over to the patrolman, "That's not his skull. He's wearing a mask."

Suddenly an expression of comprehension flashed across the motorcycle cop's face and he turned to Joe and said, "Oh no! Is it that kid around town who is always dressed in costume?"

Farmer Joe replied, "Yes that's him. His name was Charlie. He's the boy who loved Halloween."

Drooping Plywood / Gaping Windows

"Getting inside was no problem. Most of the windows were busted out and the doorways left wide open. The county had removed all the locks from the hospital to prevent curiosity seekers from getting inadvertently trapped inside. They also went through the buildings and removed every scrap of copper they could get their hands on. This meant the roof was leaky and the interior was smashed to the point where rehabilitation of the Old Asylum was no longer an option."

—from the author's private notebook

Patient Art MICA Ward

"Most of the hospital interior has been defaced by graffiti, but there are several wards where the paint on the walls predates abandonment. The Mentally Ill Chemically Addicted wing is ensconced with patient art depicting the twelve steps and the consequences of not following their tenets. Leaks caused by the stripping of the copper gutters have destroyed most of these works, but a few murals still remain as testimony to the art therapy administered when the MICA ward was still in use."

—from the author's private notebook

BLAKDRAC

ommuters traversing the decaying roads of Dirty Jersey are generally too busy honking and screaming at each other to pay much attention to the plague of graffiti whizzing past their car windows. To the streaming hordes the fading spray paint is utterly meaningless, blending together in a mush of color like a bad tattoo sleeving the landscape. For the majority of drivers and their passengers, the paint-stained wasteland rushes by in a blur, but no matter how desensitized or jaded the population has become to the writing on the wall, nobody can ignore BLAKDRAC reigning high above all others.

For years I was convinced that BLAK and DRAC were two different people. It made sense because no one person could have reached such incredible heights without an accomplice. They would have to be a team, I surmised, one person to hold the rope and belay, while the other rappelled down to paint. The graffiti lining the highways was truly an eyesore, a further blight on the already corrupted North Jersey landscape, but BLAKDRAC was different.

The rest of the population seemed to have no use for graffiti at all, looking upon it as a dirty, low-class form of expression. For me, however, the cryptic bubble letters and indecipherable scrawls were like runes of a mysterious text, hinting at the existence of secret societies and marking the demise of our decadent civilization. Esoteric gang signs and multi-colored aerosol murals in depressed cities like Paterson and Newark were the talismans I sought on my daily forays into the jungles of New Jersey. By visiting the drug-infested projects and abandoned industrial backwaters of these ghettoes, I was able to capture and amass an extensive collection of graffiti photos using my digital camera.

Very early on, when I was first starting this vandal's collage, I began entering the best of my graffiti pictures into a spreadsheet on my computer. Of course, the spreadsheet program wasn't the best way to display photos, but it had other advantages. Each line of my database was like a footnote in a book; conveying information by itself, but also furthering a larger story that would presumably require many paragraphs, chapters and sections to reveal the full meaning. As my vandal's omnibus grew, I became obsessed with the elusive tenor behind the graffiti, and this hunger for deeper wisdom drove me out on a daily basis to capture and translate the hieroglyphics of the streets.

When I would get home from one of these daily picture taking missions to my somewhat lonely one-room studio, the first thing I always did was plug my camera into the computer and upload all the day's photos. Then I would sort through the images, choosing a single photo that best represented each piece and, one by one, save them into my spreadsheet. After each tag was entered, and usually there were hundreds, I would tab through every cell, punching in the relevant data for the photos. Each line of the sheet had five columns. The first cell always contained the picture itself, which could be clicked to enlarge. The other columns were labeled: Artist, Location, Date, and Description. It was this fifth column where I spent most of my time writing out detailed observations of each graffiti piece.

As these words began to pile up, my photo database became highly searchable, allowing me to cross-reference information about individual artists and North Jersey graffiti as a whole. It also let me flush out the more visceral content of the paintings by exploring how they made me feel as I typed out my somewhat lengthy descriptions of each photo. Why I was compulsively compiling this data, I don't know, but as my spreadsheet evolved into a sprawling document, I began to see patterns emerging. There wasn't any specific message I was receiving, more of a dark mood and a dangerous aura that seemed to radiate from the data as I pored through and studied the nuances of my findings. These shadowy hints inflamed my curiosity and kept me on the case, compelling me to leave my studio each morning with fresh hope that today might be the day when I would stumble across the missing piece of the codec.

Out of all the tags I had become familiar with on my forays into the urban wilderness, no artist was more prevalent or prolific on the New Jersey scene than BLAKDRAC. Most graffiti writers content themselves with getting up along the highways or leaning out the windows of abandoned buildings with paint rollers. They rarely spray their tags above shoulder level and very few bother to use a ladder. BLAKDRAC, however, was up on the highest, most unlikely places, causing people to sometimes stop their cars and stand by the side of the road to gawk at a massive water tower or stare up at the vandalized face of a six-story brick building. Often, on my journeys into the jungles of New Jersey, I too found myself craning my neck up at the huge block letters of a BLAKDRAC tag, wondering how in the world anyone could have gotten up there to paint.

Some of the spots where BLAKDRAC hit were truly impossible, like the one on the apex of the Edgewood Road Bridge, which spans the New Jersey Turnpike and connects the town of Leonia with Englewood. After reading about the piece on the Internet, I paid a visit to the overpass, pulling over on the busy I-95 in Fort Lee to take pictures. Looking up at the massive lettering I tried to imagine how anyone could have possibly climbed up, or rappelled down to this particular spot, much less have the dexterity to paint the BLAKDRAC tag in 12-foot block font across the apex of the bridge. The underside arch proved to be such a tough spot to reach that when the state decided to remove the enormous tag, they were thwarted when their contractors couldn't find a bucket truck with a long enough arm. The DOT wasn't going to bring in a crane just to paint over some graffiti, so the tag stayed and can still be seen looming over the Turnpike to this day.

I guess it was inevitable that my obsession with the hidden meaning behind graffiti would eventually focus primarily on the BLAKDRAC tag. The ground-level scribbling on the streets and the intense muraling I encountered on my frequent trips through New Jersey's abandoned hospitals and factories spoke to me, but their message was elusive. Whatever information I received from them was always vague, offering only small clues as to what might actually be hiding behind the fabric of the jumbled words. In contrast, BLAKDRAC seemed profoundly prophetic. Although the tag was no less cagey about revealing its shadowy directive, its very boldness hinted that BLAKDRAC had more to reveal than all the other graffiti artists combined. I collected and grew my digital archive without coming across any clear answers, but never did I feel closer to my goal as when stumbling upon a fresh piece by BLAKDRAC.

It was rare, however, to discover a new BLAKDRAC before anyone else had seen it. As soon as a fresh piece would appear somewhere high above the North Jersey landscape, it would immediately be reported on by the news media. The BLAKDRAC tag was powerful in a way that others weren't. It was because of the...

Because of the what?

What was it about the BLAKDRAC tag, emblazoned so impossibly high above all the other graffiti that spoke, not just to me, but also to the population at large?

There was something about BLAKDRAC, a mood or a feeling associated with the tag that almost seemed spooky. The letters were just a little too perfect, a little too tight. When people spoke of the artist it was in a morbid tone, similar to the way they announced another terrorist strike or airline crash. News of a fresh BLAKDRAC tag seemed ominous, like a signpost of our doom or a grim reminder that our habitat has degenerated into a pollution-filled cesspool of our own making. Even for me there was something unsettling about the appearance of a new tag, but unlike others who were repelled by these cryptic messages, I was drawn to the mystery behind the bold black lettering.

I began hunting BLAKDRAC in earnest, investigating the tag in the same way the police were probably doing, but for vastly different reasons. I knew there must be more BLAKDRAC pieces that I hadn't photographed and my subsequent Internet research led me on road trips to numerous corners of New Jersey where I had not previously visited. One BLAKDRAC that I especially wanted to take a picture of could be seen while driving over the Driscol Bridge on the way down the shore. It was painted on a dilapidated water tower in the yard of a recycling company, the massive BLAKDRAC written as two words in bold black paint. After seeing pictures of the tag online, I made the trip to Keasbey, New Jersey and actually climbed the water tower in the dead of night just to get a closer look.

Going hand-over-hand up the ladder of the rusting tower was one of the scariest experiences of my life, but the detailed up-close pictures I was able to get, and the paint chip samples I collected, more than justified the terrifying climb. It was especially worth the effort because this was the only BLAKDRAC tag that I was able to get close enough to actually touch. All the others were simply impossible to access due to their height or the security at the base of the structures. For example: BLAKDRAC is notorious for painting water tanks, but except for this one particular tower in Keasbey, all the others were tightly sealed and guarded as part of the drinking water supply. After having been hit, it was always a matter of speculation in the newspapers as to how the lettering could be so large and perfect and also how the artist, or artists, could have managed to paint over the lenses of every single security camera in the area.

There seemed to be no explanation as to how BLAKDRAC was able to achieve such stealth, but I knew that if I was able to crack the mystery it would help me to decipher the hidden prophecies behind my database. After tracking down every single BLAKDRAC tag that I could find, and almost getting carjacked a few times in some bad neighborhoods, I was able to capture and enter a total of two-hundred and six BLAKDRAC tags scattered across the state, most of them in North Jersey. Analyzing the data by cross checking keywords in my spreadsheet, I began to see a pattern emerging, but couldn't quite put my finger on what steps to take next.

One snowy morning while having my first cup of coffee, an email alert arrived informing me that BLAKDRAC was in the news. I clicked on the link and was taken to a short article, only fifteen-minutes old, telling of a new BLAKDRAC tag, which had appeared on the Rutgers Street Bridge overnight. This four-lane lift-bridge spans the Passaic River between the towns of Belleville and Kearny, right next to the Arlington Diner. Later that same day, when I went to see it for myself, there was a crowd of spectators standing in the diner parking lot, staring up at a massive BLAKDRAC. It was painted as one word in huge block letters across the first tower of the powder blue bridge and could be seen all the way from the top of the hill on Route 7. I went home surging with excitement, eager to input my latest entry. The next morning, again over coffee, I received another news alert letting me know that BLAKDRAC had struck once more, this time on the side of the abandoned WR Draw which spans the Passaic River between North Newark and Kearny.

I traveled to this spot as well, struggling to find a way to access Route 21 on foot. I ended up having to walk on the abandoned rail tracks from the Newark side and climb down the icy grade of the railroad cut in order to photograph the tracks from below. As I stood there by the side of the roaring highway, taking pictures for my database, I paused to wonder how BLAKDRAC could have possibly gotten those perfect letters up there on the corroded steel of the sagging train trestle. Snapping pictures again, I was suddenly struck with an idea. I said aloud to myself, "The Rutgers Street Bridge was painted two nights ago and then on the following night this tag appeared on the WR Draw…. Maybe tonight BLAKDRAC will hit the next bridge down."

Returning home to my studio, I uploaded the images of the defaced rail crossing and then checked out a digital map to find the next bridge down from the WR Draw. It was about two miles downstream, located on the border of Kearny and East Newark. It goes by the official name of NX Bridge, but is known locally as the Annie Bridge because the towering rails were used in the dramatic final scenes of the 1982 movie where Little Orphan Annie is saved via helicopter. The NX is a defunct bascule-style crossing that is now abandoned in the open position so boats can navigate the river without obstruction. The bridge's rigid tracks permanently point up into the heavens at a sixty-five degree angle and loom high above the polluted Passaic River. I was fairly certain after doing some research on the NX that BLAKDRAC would strike again that night, so I positioned myself on the shore around dusk in a spot where I had a good view of the bridge.

Fully erect, the NX is quite phallic and clearly visible from other bridges in the area, such as the Clay Street Bridge and the Stickel Memorial Bridge, which carries Route 280 over the Passaic River. Leaving the NX open was necessary for navigation, but it has now been transformed into a monstrous eyesore that can be seen for miles when driving through Kearny, East Newark, Harrison and Newark. The area near the base of the bridge where I was sitting was actually quite dangerous at night due to crack heads and dope fiends, but I wasn't about to lose my chance of witnessing BLACDRAC in action. I had to creep my way through the homeless tents lining the abandoned rails to get there, but once I found a good perch on the cement retaining wall of the bridge I was alone and felt safe enough to settle in for a long vigil.

It was very cold that night, only about 20 degrees, but

I had come equipped for the temperature with multiple layers of clothes, a wool hat and chemical hand warmers, which I kept in the pockets of my jacket. Three or four hours passed sitting on the cold concrete with my legs dangling over the black river below. The massive rail tracks and rusting framework of the corroding bridge loomed over me like a monument to entropy, but I found myself enjoying the soothing calm of the Passaic. All was cold and quiet, the only steady sound coming from the river as it flowed against the wooden bulkhead and the crumbling cement pylons of the bridge. In the sky, the moon was full behind the elevated tracks and its brilliance merged quite beautifully with the light pollution of Newark to create a glowing crimson haze in the smog.

I regretted arriving so early, but I had not wanted to miss it if BLAKDRAC made an appearance. I kept expecting two guys with coils of rope to appear out of the darkness on the train tracks, but as midnight finally rolled around, I started to doubt they would show up. I decided to sit there for another hour or so and if they didn't arrive by one o'clock I would call it a night, because by then the cold was starting to really penetrate and I was getting restless. Just as I was about to stand up to leave I happened to glance at the bridge and saw something weird flying around against the backdrop of the red sky. It was a black shape, human in appearance, coming in fast from upriver. I sat rigid on the concrete bulkhead, my mind instinctively rejecting the information my eyes were sending into my brain. "Humans only fly in comic books and movies," I told myself. What I was seeing couldn't be real.

When it got to the bridge, the shape was still moving quickly as it began streaking in and out of the spaces between the rotting steel of the skeletal framework. It kept this up for a while, almost as if it was playing, and then I saw it fly across the river where it slowed down long enough to pause above the flat roof of a factory. The shape was too far away to see more than rudimentary details, but as it slowly descended toward the lights of the factory I could tell that the flying person I was witnessing had a distinctly feminine appearance. She approached a security camera mounted to the wall and I couldn't quite tell, but it looked like she flew down and licked the camera's lens, before abruptly flying away downstream towards the Clay Street Bridge. She spent some time down by Clay Street and I could barely see her shadowy shape flitting about the creosote piers. Just when I thought I had lost track of the spirit, if indeed spirit she was, her form came speeding up the river, twenty-feet above the shimmering black water.

She flew fast towards the NX Bridge and came to a graceful stop in a fully upright position as she hovered in front of the concrete counterweight. From my vantage point on shore I was close enough to see that the dark shape was not only female, but also possessed a remarkable beauty. She was completely black from head to toe and didn't seem to be wearing any clothes. In lieu of garments, she was ensconced in misty tendrils of gradient darkness that whispered about her and seemed to be the mysterious source of what kept her aloft. My mind still couldn't comprehend the miracle I was seeing before my eyes, but as it turned out, this strangely beautiful creature had more surprises in store for the night.

After surveying the counterweight to her satisfaction, she began levitating in a horizontal position almost as if she was lying on her stomach. She then flew to the left corner of the weight where I watched her hover in close to the concrete, stopping with her face only inches from the surface. Then, without touching the wall with her hands, she stuck out her tongue and began licking. From my vantage point I had a good angle and could see her incredibly long tongue running against the wall, leaving behind a thick coat of black paint. As I watched, I could see that her tongue was far superior to any brush humans could have made. The lines it left behind on the rough concrete went on smoother than even the creamiest interior wall paint on the market today. After every few licks, her tongue would retract back into her mouth and then emerge again, freshly loaded like a wet brush from a paint can, but infinitely quicker and a thousand times more exact. Sometimes she would pause at her licking to fly backwards so she could get a wider perspective on her lettering. Once satisfied, she would zip back to the wall and enthusiastically resume her work.

As the outline of the first few letters began to take shape under her rapidly maneuvering tongue, there was no doubt in my mind that this exotic creature was BLAK-DRAC. As I watched her graceful performance, she hovered before her concrete canvas, flicking that enchanted tongue with the assurance and confidence of an accomplished artist. I sat in awe on my perch, too scared to move and too spellbound to tear my eyes away from this aerial virtuoso. I wanted to reach for my camera, but was so terrified of this supernatural being that I scarcely dared to breathe, lest she sense my presence. But oh how wrong I was on that point. As she finished her piece and flew back to survey her work for one last time, I saw her glance casually in my direction with a smirk as if she had known I was there the whole time.

In an instant she flew over to where I was sitting on the concrete retaining wall, my legs still dangling over the river. One moment she was hovering thirty-feet away and the next second she was floating with her face six-inches from mine, those shadowy tendrils lapping against my winter clothes and tickling my face. I was truly scared, but the hypnotizing elegance of the creature kept me from looking away. Her eyes were glowing emerald green and in the moonlight her face looked statuesque, as if she had been carved from a glistening slab of ebony marble. I didn't know if I was going to fall in love with her or run screaming into the night, but before I could do anything she gave me a slight smile, which froze me to the spot. As I sat there transfixed, she stuck out her incredibly long tongue and gently licked the bridge of my nose, leaving behind a perfect stripe of black-painty-goo. With that, she whooshed off silently into the night, zipping over her freshly painted BLAKDRAC tag, maneuvering through the beams of the NX Bridge and then silhouetting herself against the moon before disappearing into the darkness.

I was so dazed by my experience at the bridge that I can barely remember how I managed to get home. Ever since I saw her, I have existed in an absent-minded fog, completely neglecting my essential needs and shirking even my most basic responsibilities. Performing rudimentary tasks such as brushing my teeth, eating food, or reading a book has lost all meaning to me. My mind is still struggling to compute and categorize the occurrences I witnessed at the NX Bridge and the beautiful BLAKDRAC is all I can think about. The only photographic record I have from that night is the selfie I took when I got home. It's of me, standing in front of my bathroom mirror, still wearing all my winter clothes and sporting a thick stripe of black paint down the bridge of my nose. I have finally gotten myself together enough to sit down in front of my machine and enter the photo into my spreadsheet as evidence. I am now writing out this long description in the fifth column of the database where you are no doubt reading it for yourself. I have fallen in love with the creature who calls herself BLAKDRAC. I must find her again and I will use the data in this spreadsheet to do so. I still haven't cracked the code behind New Jersey's cryptic graffiti, but as long as she's out there painting I'll be on the hunt.

Wheelchair with Amputee Ghost

"There was a legless amputee who lived here for many years. Every day he would park his wheelchair at the end of the ward and watch the door. He was looking for an opportunity to elope, but each time the door opened he was too slow to escape. He was a very quiet man and rarely spoke. Eventually he just became part of the furniture, so to speak. One day he died in his chair waiting for the door to open. Nobody noticed until bed check. He never did make it through that door because they took him out the back, but I guess he managed to escape in his own way."

—from a patient diary left behind on the wards

Seduction Instructions

Climb through the fence of the Old Asylum. Peep through the bushes for cops. The coast is clear. Scramble up the fire escape to the fifth floor. Peel the plywood back from the doorway. Disappear into the building. Duck under the electrical wires. Hurry to the last door on the left. This is the room with the view. Walk to the window. Caress the underside of the sill with your hand.

Searching... Searching... Found it. Unwrap the cellophane stash. Spark up the roach from last week. This is good weed. It burns slow. Feel the smoke. Love the smoke. It's starting to burn your fingers. Gather a little saliva on your tongue. Pop the last nub of burning paper into your mouth. Eat the evidence. Now, you're ready. This adventure is about to begin.

Light up a cigarette and head into the hallway. Ignore the slamming doors on the lower floors. You know it's just the wind. Stop to read some new graffiti. *666 SATAN LOVES YOU*. Chuckle to yourself. Walk to the interior stairwell. Take the steps two at time. Jump off the landing and ninja-kick the door. Shudder with satisfaction as the deafening boom echoes through the abandoned asylum. Walk down the first floor hallway. Feel your boots squish on wet carpet. Pick up a can of discarded spray paint. Shake it. Just a dry rattle. Don't worry. Your cans are stashed below.

Kick in the door to the basement. Approach the stairwell. Pause for a moment. Smell the rot. Taste the mildew. Breathe in the warm subterranean draft. Swallow your natural fear of the dark. Flick the Zippo. Descend. Don't look at the cave crickets. Keep your eyes on the rickety stairs. Cup the lighter against the draft. Move quickly through the soggy basement.

The third door on your right is the medical supply room. Wedge it open with a discarded enema bag. Hurry! The lighter is getting hot. Go to the closet on the far side of the room. Do you remember where you saw the Shroud Kits? There they are. Try not to touch the mildewed box as you fish one out. This is taking too long. The Zippo is unbearably hot. OK you got it. One Shroud Kit. Retreat from the room in haste. Down the hallway. Up the stairs. Blink in the daylight as you emerge from the basement. Sigh with relief in the safety of the sun. Proceed to the third floor of the Old Asylum. Here comes the creative part of your mission.

Throw open the door to room sixty-six. Let out a spontaneous squeal of joy at the task you are about to perform. Grab your supplies from where you stashed them in the closet. Open the Shroud Kit package and read the directions. *Place deceased on shroud sheet with cellulous pad under rectum.* Follow the instructions. Spread the shroud sheet on the hospital bed in front of you. The corpse you're creating isn't real. If you're going to fool anybody you have to make it perfect. Grab the pants from the box of supplies. They're already stuffed tight with packing peanuts. Take the rag-stuffed sweatshirt from the box. Grab the duct tape and attach the shirt to the waistband of the pants. Now you have a body.

Pull out the battered pair of Converse All Stars. Tape the sneakers in place where the feet should go. Your carcass is almost complete. Reach into the box for the mannequin head. Laugh quietly to yourself as you duct tape it to the torso. Glance back at the Shroud Kit directions.

Fasten chinstrap, protecting face with cellulose pad. Should you skip this process? The mannequin head doesn't need a chinstrap. Decide to be thorough. Place the cellulose pad over the Styrofoam mouth. Wrestle the chinstrap in place. Move on to the next step.

Fold arms over abdomen. Tie wrists and ankles. The arms of your dummy won't be visible under the sheet. Use the duct tape instead of the ties. Rip off a long piece of tape and wrap the arms together. You're having fun now. You're thinking of her reaction. Take another look at the instructions.

Tie shroud above elbows, at waist, and below knees. Make sure you perform this step with meticulous precision. This is the part that really counts. You want your corpse to look real. Fold the shroud over the dummy's body. Tighten the strings around the shroud. Tie the body up like a package. Your peanut-stuffed corpse is looking pretty authentic. Wrap up the details. Adjust the legs. Make them look rigid and straight. Tighten the ties around the torso. Nudge the head into the perfect position.

Oh no! Suddenly you remember the blood. Step back and look at the corpse. Wish that you hadn't forgotten to grab your red spray paint from the basement. Now you don't have anything to use for fake blood. Shake your head in disappointment. Should you go back down? No time for that. Better get this job done before sundown.

Deal with the blood situation. This body needs some gore. Pull the straight razor out of your boot. Flick the blade. Don't hesitate. Slice open your wrist just above the tattoo. Whoah! Easy cowboy! Don't slice too deep. Yeah, there you go. Plenty of blood. Drip it on the shroud. Right on the face. Now smear some blood on the crotch. Don't let the cellulose rectum pad go to waste. Squeeze your arm. Push the blood from the wound. Make it flow. Come on now. This has to look real.

OK good. That's enough. A real artist knows when to stop painting. Slap a length of duct tape over the slash wound on your wrist. Roll down your sleeve. Ignore the pain in your throbbing forearm. Step back. Contemplate the finished product. Grab the supply box. Shove it in the closet. Take one last look at your corpse. Make a few adjustments to the legs. Chuckle to yourself. Close the door on room sixty-six.

Proceed down the stairs. Out the gate. Back to your car. Laugh the whole way home. Park your car. Run inside your apartment. Check your messages. Call Jessica. Confirm your dinner date. Take a shower. Wash the cut on your arm with antibacterial soap. Towel off. Dress the wound. It isn't so bad. Look at the clock. You're running late. You have to pick up Jess in twenty minutes. Drape yourself in black. Slick back your mohawk. No time to spike it. Slap patchouli all over yourself. Run out the door with a huge smile on your face.

Swing by Jess's house and park in the driveway. Knock on the door and give her mother a kiss on the cheek. Accept the invitation to come inside. Behold Jess as she descends the stairs. Is she the one? Don't worry. Tonight will be the test. Buy her dinner at a fancy restaurant. Take her to a movie. *Blair Witch* is on the silver screen. Let the film set the mood. Make out with her afterwards. Sit in your car and pass a joint. You don't want to go home. Neither does she.

This is the moment you have been waiting for. Tell her about the Old Asylum. Describe the vandalized hallways. Paint her a mental picture of the abandoned psychiatric hospital. She wants to go. She wants to see it. Your plan is working nicely.

Drive to the outskirts of the Old Asylum. Park your car in a hidden grotto. Kill the engine and enter the woods. Suddenly there are bright lights in the trees. Jessica grabs your arm. Pull her down into the bushes. A policeman's searchlight dances above your heads. Huddle with her in the prickers. Stare into her eyes. Feel your hearts beating in sync. Watch the cruiser roll slowly off the property.

Breathe a sigh of relief. Turn back to Jessica. Her eyes want you to kiss her. Taste her lips. Touch her tongue. Lose yourself in her mouth. Ok, this is fun. Take Jess's hand. Lead her through the hole in the fence. Turn on your flashlight. Make sure the beam is always at her feet. Ignore the fire escape. Enter through the basement. This isn't the door you used earlier. This is the morgue. Feel the midnight cold of the air. Enjoy the surge of power as Jessica grips your hand ever tighter.

Flash the beam of light over the autopsy tables. Point out the sliding trays of the morgue drawers. Show her the piles of medical waste stacked against the wall. Point the flashlight into the room on your left. Pan the light over hundreds of used hypodermic needles carpeting the floor. Look into Jessica's eyes and gauge her fear. She seems pretty scared. Maybe this wasn't a good idea. Ask her if she's okay. Smile as she gives you a hesitant nod. Tell her the upper floors are a lot less scary. Lead her through the cavernous basement hallway. Locate the stairs. Ascend.

Suddenly a tremendous boom rolls through the building. Jess nearly jumps out of her skin. She clings to your back. Her breath is frantic in your ear. Ease her fears. Console her. Explain to her about the draft in this place. "It's just the wind slamming doors." She trusts you. Your words have comforted her. Lead her out of the stairwell. Give her a tour of the lower floors. Watch her marvel at the wreckage. She's never been in an abandoned hospital before.

Show her the main kitchen with its smashed plates and dishes. Pull open the doors to the walk in freezer. Tell her about the corpses that were stored here. Show her the staff quarters. The chapel. The shock therapy rooms. Expose the darkened sanitarium. Invite her into your favorite world.

Marvel at Jessica's boldness now that her fear has passed. Soon it will be time to bring her up to room sixty-six. She's almost ready. Take her hand. Lead her up the stairs to the third floor. Moonlight flows in through the broken windows. It's much brighter up here. Switch the flashlight off. Jess isn't scared anymore. She's laughing and bubbling. She tells you that she's never felt so alive. Smile at her. Squeeze her hand. Lead her further down the hall.

Wait a second. What was that noise? She turns and stares at you. "Did you hear that?" You definitely heard it. The sound of many sneaker-clad feet. Voices somewhere on the lower floors. Teenage laughter rolls up the elevator shaft. You are not alone in the Old Asylum. Jess is scared. "Let's just get out of here."

You're pissed off. This ruins your plan. The sound of drunken laughter is getting closer. The people are coming up the stairs. You smile at Jess and say, "I have a confession to make..." Tell her the whole story in quiet whispers. Tell her how you made the corpse and covered it with the shroud sheet. Tell her how you plotted to scare her. Tell her how you sliced your arm to get the blood. Explain everything in short, abbreviated sentences.

Glance at the stairwell. The voices are closer. Observe the wonder in her eyes. Scrutinize her unexpected smile. "You did all that for me? No one has ever done anything like that for me. This is so romantic."

Did you hear her correctly? This girl is definitely the one. The footsteps are almost at the landing. You can see the flashlight beams in the hallway. Grab Jessica's arm. Pull her into room sixty-six. The kids are on the third floor now. Listen close at the door. Try to separate the shrill sounds. How many of them are there? Judging by the noise there seems to be five or six. Turn your flashlight off. Glance at Jess. She is crouching by the bed admiring your handiwork. She's running her hand over the shrouded corpse. She whispers to you, "I know I should be mad, but this is such a beautiful gesture. None of my other boyfriends understood me like this."

The voices and footsteps are getting closer. Three rooms down someone slams a door. High fives and choruses of laughter are heard through the walls. Jess is nervous again. She stands up and moves close by your side. "What if they come in here?" Smile at Jess. Fix her with your most devilish stare. The room next door is filled with the sound of teenage laughter. There will be no avoiding these kids. They are coming.

Take Jess by the shoulders. Lead her to the far side of the hospital bed. Stand side by side over the shrouded corpse. Brush the purple streaks out of her eyes. She appears demonic in the moonlight. Imagine what you must look like. Squeeze Jessica's hand.

You can hear the kids blundering back into the hallway. Muffled laughter rings through the wall. They're psyched up. Someone smashes a bottle outside. BOOM! The door is kicked open. They stand before you in a mob. Their flashlights blaze in your face. Don't flinch. Keep your eyes locked. Stare into the lights. The group's laughter is abruptly silenced. Smile at them. Let them see the psychotic couple standing over the shrouded body. Watch as the image soaks into their brains.

The seconds tick by. Finally one of them screams. The wayward explorers break from their paralysis. They bolt down the hallway. Shrieks echo through the Old Asylum. Jess falls into your arms. She's laughing uncontrollably. Tip your head back and howl along with her. Plant a big kiss on her forehead. Give her a huge hug. There is no doubt about it. She is the one. The joy in your heart is complete.

Waiting Area at the Old Asylum Morgue

"An inmate suffering from severe catalepsy was misdiagnosed as dead after she was discovered rigid on the floor of her padded cell. She woke hours later in the morgue drawer. When she was finally extracted from the cooler, all her fingernails were pulled back and bleeding from attempting to scratch her way out. Hospital staff tried to keep the incident a secret, but a funeral director happened to be in the waiting area when the screaming started. Word got around and there was a full investigation by the state. No one was charged and business went on as usual."

—from an email exchange with a former staff member

Basement Corridor of the Old Asylum

"When I was an orderly at the Old Asylum, one hallway always scared me and sent chills down my spine. It was in the basement and there was this huge brown splotch on the wall that looked like dried blood, as if someone had committed suicide with a shotgun. You know, really blew their brains all over the wall. I went back after the hospital was abandoned just to see the place and the stain was still there. Shortly after seeing the blood I got spooked and left. Honestly, if I never go back to that place it will be too soon. Some of the stuff I saw there will haunt me to the grave."

—from an email exchange with a former staff member

SIX SIX SIX

The Old Asylum had been shamefully neglected for decades. The soggy walls couldn't take another coat of paint and the roof leaked so profusely that the inmates sometimes woke during the night in flooded cells. The county administrators had been ignoring the issue for years, but when it became profitable to repurpose the land for condominiums the bureaucrats suddenly made a fuss about "patient rights" and began lobbying for funds to replace the Old Asylum.

Once the necessary monies were in hand, the county slapped together a new mental hospital down the hill and prepared to transfer the patients from the Old Asylum. The new hospital was touted to be an ultra-modern psychiatric care clinic with room for expansion, but from the outset, the facility was woefully inadequate for the challenges it was about to face. As the new hospital construction was finalized, Hastur Chambers published his book *SIX SIX SIX* to an unsuspecting public. There was an irresistible draw to the text that caused the title to become an unprecedented bestseller, but as a rule, any person who dared read the dread book, was driven permanently insane.

No lucid person of sound mind can understand why people become violently demented when they read *SIX SIX SIX*. Anyone who reads the book invariably goes mad within the first few pages. Although *SIX SIX SIX* has been studied from afar, there hasn't yet been anyone capable of getting through the text without stabbing stigmata into their hands and descending into psychotic derangement. Despite the known dangers, the print edition of the book quickly became a runaway bestseller. The digital version of *SIX SIX SIX* went "viral" and was passed around for free on the Internet, causing innocent victims to go mad simply by opening their email and reading the unsolicited text. The widespread distribution of the *SIX SIX SIX* book caused an influx of psychotic patients to flood health care systems around the globe and the freshly painted wards of the new county facility were overwhelmed along with the rest. The outbreak of *SIX SIX SIX* madness was particularly severe in New York City where Hastur Chambers lived and where the book first debuted. As the book's influence spread, the new psychiatric hospital located only nineteen miles from the epicenter of the outbreak, was soon filled beyond its intended capacity. As a result, the county executives were not able to decommission the Old Asylum the way they had originally planned. The *SIX SIX SIX* plague was upon them.

As a means of disassociating the new hospital from the Old Asylum, the new psychiatric facility had been constructed on a detached parcel of land located down the hill. Before the *SIX SIX SIX* outbreak began, contracts had been put in place to rip down the Old Asylum buildings once and for all. Condominium developers were waiting in the wings to construct cheap housing at huge profits and the bulldozers were gassed up and ready to go. The sale was touted as a lucrative deal for everyone involved and shifting off site was also a public relations ploy. They wanted the new hospital to be completely cut off from the notoriously barbaric mental health care that had been practiced behind the locked doors of the Old Asylum for more than a century.

From a business standpoint the land deal made sense, but the slick politicians and fast-talking construction moguls hadn't accounted for the mass psychosis that was about to infect a large cross-section of their constituents. When it started, first in North America and then across the world, municipalities and governments struggled to play catch up with their mental health care facilities. As the book's readership climbed into the multi-millions, the *SIX SIX SIX* psychosis contaminated large swaths of the world's population. In the Garden State, the people of New Jersey were not immune to the effects of the literary madness. As the new hospital quickly filled to capacity, it became clear that the Old Asylum would have to remain open in order to absorb the excess patients overtaking the wards. Instead of full coffers from a juicy land sale, the county found itself burdened with a crowded morgue, two overflowing psychiatric hospitals, and a mental health care crisis of biblical proportions.

Even before the *SIX SIX SIX* epidemic had begun, many people expressed the opinion that the new county psychiatric hospital was shamefully long overdue. By every known standard, the ancient wards should have been dismantled decades ago, but except for the wings that have fallen down on their own, the Old Asylum stands to this day. It's said to be a haunted place and the buildings look the part with their broken windows, unkempt grounds and sagging slate roofs. The towering red brick exteriors of the massive institution are choked with creeping poison ivy vines. Jimson Weed thrives in abundance at the base of the antediluvian wards. Praying mantis and butterflies have reclaimed what were once mowed lawns and manicured courtyards.

The earliest structures on the Old Asylum property date back to the late 1800's and the sanitarium looks as if it materialized straight out of the pages of a Victorian ghost story. The elements have not been kind to the structures and, although the asylum might look picturesque to some from the outside, few would find the hallways of the locked wards to be appealing. Everything under those leaking slate roofs is rotten, moldy, dark, and cavernous. Continuing to treat patients at the Old Asylum was not ideal, but the *SIX SIX SIX* plague had left the county with no choice. Most wings of the Old Asylum were too far gone to be of any use, but there was one building that was just serviceable enough to pass state inspections. This lone edifice was the Reception building, which had been opened in 1942 as an addition to the Administration wing.

The Reception wing is a four story brick fortress connected to the main hospital by an ornate bridge that spans a courtyard between the two structures. Unlike the rest of the Old Asylum, Reception has a flat rubber roof that leaks a bit during a hard rain, but not nearly as much as the slate roofs on the older wards. As the plaster walls of the sanitarium gradually decayed from frequent soakings, the staff had been forced to retreat across the enclosed bridge to the Reception building. This was the only dry spot left in the hospital and although the four wards of Reception were quite large, it was a tight fit to squeeze all the patients.

Once the staff had lugged all their medical equipment and files across the long hallway, the doctors locked the doors behind them in an attempt to block out the creeping decay. From that moment on, Reception became the last holdfast against insanity on the Old Asylum grounds.

Once the new hospital down the hill was in operation, the last remaining wards of the Old Asylum were supposed to have been emptied, but that's not how things worked out. Presently, Reception still has its lights on and is now widely known as the "Book Club" because all four floors are dedicated to the housing of *SIX SIX SIX* victims.

In an attempt to discover the most effective treatment for this literary mind plague, scientists around the world started pooling their data in hopes of finding a cure. Despite the consequences of reading *SIX SIX SIX*, nefarious publishing companies and unscrupulous web trolls continue to disseminate the book in numerous languages. These releases are always met with protests, manhunts, and public book burnings, but *SIX SIX SIX* has a mysterious way of bubbling up from the underground and getting into people's hands. Outbreaks of *SIX SIX SIX* psychosis have been reported in almost every major city in the world, cementing the fact that the problem isn't merely local, but global. The doctors at the Old Asylum were some of the first researchers to begin participating in the collective experiment to find a cure. Based on preliminary findings and recommendations from scientists abroad, they have rearranged Reception into 4 separate wards, assigning each floor its own directive for treating the effects of the *SIX SIX SIX* book.

The first floor, E-Ward, is the electroconvulsive therapy floor where the most hopeless cases are routinely electrocuted in an attempt to shock their brains back to reality. The second floor, F-Ward, is for family therapy, where husbands, wives, and even children affected by the book can share a room while they try to heal. The third floor, T-Ward, is reserved for talk therapy and is the only wing in the entire hospital where patients are allowed to discuss the book. The fourth floor, L-Ward, has been transformed into a maximum-security lockdown, where the most violent and unruly patients are kept restrained for 23 hours a day.

If the bridge hallway between Administration and Reception hadn't been permanently locked, the heavy steel doors would have opened directly onto the T-Ward day room. When the entirety of the hospital was still in operation both sets of doors stayed latched in the open position all day long. This would allow a cross breeze of fresh air to blow between the Administration wing and the Reception wards. Now, with the doors permanently barred, the air on T-Ward is always thick and stagnant no matter how many windows are propped open or fans kept running. During the summertime T-Ward roasts in the heat. The only cool place on the entire floor is by the doorway to the bridge, where a slight trickle of air still flows under the barrier. It's an attractive spot to sit and rest, but Book Club patients are forbidden from lingering there. The doctors don't want them sneaking a look through the reinforced glass windows and seeing something that might upset them: such as a rat, a trespassing teenager or maybe even a ghost.

The seemingly endless hallway down the middle of the building is lined with tiny isolation cells from one end of the ward to the other. At night, every one of the cells has an occupant, but presently the patients are assembled in the day room. It's group therapy time and there's a guest speaker on the ward.

"They say the apocalypse is upon us, but I'm not so sure as I once was. When I pictured it before I thought it would be like a huge bang or an explosion and we would all be whisked out into space or something and the sinners would just get wiped away. But this is different. This is a personal apocalypse as much as it is a collapse of our civilization. I never thought my life would change so drastically from simply reading a book, and if it did, I guess I assumed it would be from the Bible and it would be a good change. I have no history of mental illness in my family and I've never touched an illegal drug in my life. This sickness has taken me totally by surprise, and as I'm sure you all can relate, completely devastated my family."

It was almost unbearably stagnant and smelly in the sweltering day room. Thirty cigarettes burned in thirty stigmata scarred hands as the drugged and drooling patients of T-Ward listened to the slow drawl of the lady behind the rickety podium. Her name was Marjory and she was one of the very rare *SIX SIX SIX* patients to be sent home on an outpatient basis. She was a "graduate" of the new facility down the hill and was only released because of her strong household support. The drugs in her system kept her fairly stable as long as her family was around, but she was nervous at the podium and it caused her to obsessively rub the scars on her hands. Glancing at her husband seated in the back of the room, Marjory squinted through the haze of smoke and sputtered a little as she paused in her sharing. After a brief coughing spell, she apologized saying, "I'm sorry I'm not used to all this smoke. We weren't allowed cigarettes down the hill and I'm not a smoker anyhow." This left her listeners nonplussed and a disapproving sigh passed through the crowd.

Smoking was strictly forbidden at the fancy new hospital, but not in the Old Asylum. The ancient Reception building was unquestionably more of a firetrap than the modern institution down the hill, but tobacco was such a firm tradition at the decaying Old Asylum that nobody could imagine this as a smoke free zone. From a curative standpoint, banning cigarettes here on the talk therapy ward was almost unthinkable. The hourly smoke breaks were the only bright spots for many of the patients as they spent long, torturous days sitting on the mental ward. This was actually Marjory's first time inside the Old Asylum and it made her feel uncomfortable. She didn't want to mention it, but as she looked at her surroundings she was grateful that she had been in the new psychiatric facility down the hill. She couldn't imagine spending even one night in this spooky sanitarium with its smoky rooms, cockroach corners, and tattered dusty drapes. There was a smell of sickness here that bit deep into her nostrils and Marjory shuddered a bit as she stared out into the sea of sad blank faces.

"I'm so grateful to the doctors and the staff for counseling me through my delusions and finding the right combination of medications to help me get my life back." She wasn't a particularly rousing speaker, but that was probably for the best. It's not good to get the patients too riled up and Marjory was just about the right speed for this crew. Also, it helped that she was on the same medication as most of the folks in her audience. Their fragile brains were moving at a similar pace and she held their attention despite the droning cadence of her words. As she described her reading of the book and her subsequent mental collapse, there were a few murmurs from the crowd as the other patients found themselves identifying with her story.

Ambrose watched from his seat in the back of the room, his legs crossed as he leaned on his clipboard and scanned the back of the group's heads for signs of disturbance or agitation. When Marjory finally began wrapping up her story, the inmates perked up a little as she described her current life on the outside. "Luckily, my husband and my sons aren't really the literary types so they never read *SIX SIX SIX*, which is ironic, considering how much I used to try to encourage them to read books. They've been so supportive and have even removed all the sharp objects, televisions, and computer devices from our home so I don't have to ever be exposed to any images of the book or be confronted by those words again. I do my best to keep my blinders on like the doctors down the hill taught me and we're still praying for my beautiful daughter who unfortunately did read the book and is currently down the hill in a se-se-se-segregation cell."

Marjory's lower lip began quivering as she described her daughter, and even though Ambrose wasn't her counselor, he could tell from experience that she was about to have a "setback" as they call it on the wards. Ambrose stood up in the back of the room, his authoritative voice breaking the tension in the air as he said, "Let's all thank Marjory, who has come such a long way from when she was first admitted down the hill. I hope all of you listened carefully to her story because there is a lot to learn from the outpatients, and Marjory is one of our most exciting success stories. She brought you a profound message of hope today and I want to thank you Marjory for having the courage to get up in front of T-Ward and offer us the gift of your story. Let's all give Marjory a round of applause." A subdued clapping was all the group could muster, but it sufficed to lift Marjory's spirits a little. She was smiling through her tears as she made her way back to her husband and sons, who had been seated on the sidelines, and had tears in their eyes as well.

Behind his authoritative pose, Ambrose sighed deeply and steeled himself before opening his mouth again, lest the patients sense his malaise. He was a relatively new doctor at the hospital and shouldn't have been weary of his career just yet, but the futility of his work was beginning to take a toll. He could sense hopelessness in the body language of every one of his patients, and as they stood up at his eventual command to get in line, he let out a deep sigh. Before the door was unlocked, the nurses performed a head count and then Ambrose supervised as the pathetic horde shuffled single file down the stairs for an hour of caged-in recreation time. Outdoors, in the harsh light of the August sun, the group looked even more forlorn than they had on the ward. The *SIX SIX SIX* victims were a sad sight to behold and it broke Ambrose's heart to see his Camilla among them.

His patients were mixed gender and of dissimilar backgrounds, but the one thing they all had in common was that they lost their minds while reading *SIX SIX SIX*. Ambrose's training told him that the best way to treat the victims of this literary pestilence was to group them together and let them talk about the problem, but the more he listened to the inmates tell their stories, the less he was sure. For one thing, he couldn't figure out why anyone would read *SIX SIX SIX* at all when the dangers were so widely known. It was said that the book had a way of luring its readers even when they knew the risk, but Ambrose just couldn't bring himself to believe that a book could have *that* much power. Another puzzling aspect to the *SIX SIX SIX* phenomenon was that even though they had all been driven crazy by the same text, none of the victims could agree on what the book was actually about. As he babysat his inmates in the cage, Ambrose reflected that he had been hired as much for his doctorate in psychology as he was for his brawny build. Fights broke out constantly during talk therapy when patients failed to find common ground and

Ambrose had to step in on a daily basis when the arguments inevitably turned physical. After a long shift on T-Ward, he usually left for the day feeling that the men and women in his care were beyond hope.

Ambrose had never read *SIX SIX SIX* himself, nor had any other sane man or woman who wanted to keep their marbles. Apparently it was impossible to read the text without descending into madness. As of yet no one could clinically prove why the book was so destructive because anyone examining the pages for clues invariably went insane. Ambrose hadn't been swept away by the viral trend that *SIX SIX SIX* created, but his girlfriend Camilla had been one of the earliest victims. On the day of the tragedy, Camilla had been in good spirits and appeared to be perfectly normal. She cooked their breakfast and kissed Ambrose on the cheek as he was leaving for class. It was the last day of school before finalizing his degree and they were both excited for Ambrose to finish up. In two days they were scheduled to embark on a trip to the Caribbean that Ambrose's parents had generously bestowed upon them as a graduation present. Camilla had taken the day off from her job at the bookstore and started her vacation a little early. Her plan was to wash the breakfast dishes and then spend the rest of the morning luxuriously reading on the balcony.

When he returned home that evening, Ambrose discovered Camilla naked in the hall closet of their apartment. She had gaping stigmata wounds on the palms of each hand and the tips of several of her fingers were gnawed to the bone. Her entire body was drenched in gore and jagged claw marks ran down her face where she had tried to scratch out her eyes. Camilla had been screaming herself raw behind the locked door and when he wrenched it open, Ambrose initially mistook her for a deranged stranger in the house.

When he finally forced himself to believe that this was indeed his girlfriend, he dialed 911 and the ambulance arrived to take her to the hospital. After several surgeries and months of healing she was released, but not to the outside world. Her mind had been scarred beyond repair and she was no longer able to function in society. Camilla was committed to the new county psychiatric hospital for thirty days so the doctors could evaluate her mental state. When her monitoring was complete, she was diagnosed with Unspecified Psychotic Disorder and permanently transferred to T-Ward on the Old Asylum.

Ambrose loved his girlfriend very much and was understandably distraught by her traumatic personality shift. He staunchly visited Camilla every day of the week and always stayed past normal visiting times. The nurses were sympathetic to his devotion and they let him linger after hours without ever saying a word. The doctors at the hospital also appreciated Ambrose's dedication and when they found out that he held a doctorate in psychology, they immediately begged him to accept a position on the staff. Ambrose had been neglecting his financial responsibilities ever since Camilla took ill and hadn't thought much about looking for a job, but the idea appealed to him. Using the county's staffing crisis as leverage, he agreed to practice at the hospital, but only if he would be assigned to Camilla's ward. Normally this concession would not have been granted, but the administration desperately needed a qualified psychologist to run the talk therapy floor at the Old Asylum. Once he officially had the job, Ambrose began putting in grueling seventy-hour work weeks just to be with Camilla for as long as possible each day.

As he watched his other patients shuffling aimlessly about the yard, Ambrose's eyes fell on Camilla who was in her usual spot by the corner of the fence. She was crouched there rocking back and forth, and observing this, Ambrose hoped it was only a side effect of her medicine, not an indication of her progressing mental illness. He made his way to her across the cracked and weedy asphalt, being careful not to get too close as he crouched down beside her. She didn't like to be touched anymore and Ambrose was sensitive to that fact. Cigarette smoke hung in the hot summer air, but it didn't seem to bother Camilla even though she was one of the few patients who didn't partake. Ambrose almost wished she did smoke because at least it would animate her body and give her something to do besides staring off into space. She had barely spoken over the last several months and as he watched her swaying in place Ambrose feared, not for the first time, that her psychosis was slipping into a state of catatonia.

Camilla's long red hair, that had once been so striking and vibrant, hung about her face like a bad wig and was now as brittle and dry as a bird's nest. The once lovely freckles splashed across her cheeks stood out like sores amongst the scars on her pale blank face. It damn near killed Ambrose just to look at her. As she rocked back and forth he suddenly noticed that a host of mosquitoes had landed on her papery skin and were growing fat as they sucked her blood. Seeing this, Ambrose sought to wave away the insects by flapping his hands around Camilla's face and although his actions were enough to make the bugs take flight, Camilla's eyes never even blinked. "Honey let's get up and go inside. Rec time is almost over and you're getting eaten alive out here." The once beautiful Camilla said nothing and made no indication that she had heard the man whom she had once loved. Ever so gently he touched her elbow and used a single index finger to guide her into a standing position. Camilla passively stood up and shuffled along beside Ambrose as he led her slowly back upstairs into the dayroom of the Old Asylum.

Camilla sat as directed in a dayroom chair and Ambrose pulled his own chair closer to examine the bites. Large welts were forming on her sensitive skin, but she didn't scratch or move a muscle to relieve the itch. Ambrose felt a lump forming in his throat and choked back a sob. It was the little things like mosquito bites and lack of hygiene that really showed her degeneration. Each time he noticed her taking another step towards mental oblivion, it cut him deeply. As the rest of the patients began trickling back upstairs, Ambrose wiped a bit of moisture from his eyes and tried to prepare himself for the rest of the day. To his dismay he found that he was not able to do it.

Suddenly the walls were closing in and the thought of being trapped on the ward for the next round of group sessions was too much to bear. Anxiety flared up his spine and he broke into a panic sweat that covered every inch of his body. Ambrose stood up in an effort to regain control, not wanting his nurses or his patients to see him crying, but he could tell it was a losing battle. He tried to hold back the tears, but as he looked down at Camilla's face, a deep sob burst forth unwillingly from his lungs. This sudden involuntary convulsion caused snot to shoot out of his nose and to his horror, a yellow ball of mucus landed directly on Camilla's forehead. She didn't even bat an eyelid as the trail of slime traced a path down her pale skin and settled in the corner of her mouth. Seeing this, Ambrose let out another anguished cry of despair from deep in his diaphragm. Moaning, he fumbled with a handkerchief to wipe the snot from Camilla's face and once it was clean, ran hysterically out of the room.

On the way down the stairs he met Linda, his most competent and experienced nurse. She looked concerned to see him so upset, but not overly surprised. All the staff had observed the personal strain Ambrose had been under since coming to work as his girlfriend's doctor. Nurse Linda felt a maternal sympathy for him as he ran weeping past her, but she let him go without interfering. She could see what was bothering Ambrose and she knew there were no words capable of easing his suffering. Down in the cage, Ambrose fumbled with the keys on his ring and finally located the ancient skeleton key that unlatched the gate of T-Ward's recreation yard. Through a haze of tears he managed to open the fence and lock it again behind him. After tearing blindly through prickers and tall grass, Ambrose emerged onto what was left of *Sanitarium Road*, now no more than two tire tracks pressed into the weedy brush.

Still sobbing, Ambrose shoved his hands deep into his suit pockets and walked blindly towards the abandoned sections of the hospital. Stomping forward with angry steps, he had no specific destination in mind except to escape. Feeling the need to justify his sudden departure he said aloud, "I just had to get the hell off T-Ward for a few minutes, maybe an hour. Oh, but Camilla is in there. Why, god, why?" Up ahead, two nurses sat on a bench just off the decaying road. They were enjoying cigarettes and had the remains of their lunch neatly piled on the bench between them. Both ladies greeted Ambrose as he approached, but were cut short when they saw his upset face. He had a sudden impulse to stop and cry on their shoulders, but there was something in their guarded posture that wouldn't allow for it. He feebly nodded as he passed them and the women sympathetically returned his greeting, but didn't say another word. They were nurses after all; they knew that look.

Past the lunching nurses, the Old Asylum grounds grew thick and dark under the lush canopy of encroaching forest that shaded the hospital grounds. Ambrose hadn't been this deep into the sanitarium property since he was a kid riding bikes with his friends, but any sense of nostalgia eluded him. As he passed through the small city of dilapidated mental wards he barely even looked up at his ominous surroundings. *Sanitarium Road* led him past the crumbling Female Wing and the Back Male Ward where an unseen raven watched Ambrose's progress from atop a corroded copper cupola. Peculiar shadows flickered across dusty windows as he passed the vacant chapel of the Old Asylum and odd shuffling sounds emanated from behind the locked vestibule. Normally he would have been scared out of his mind to tread here, but none of the unusual stimuli in the haunted asylum registered with Ambrose. All he could think about was Camilla sitting silently on T-Ward with mosquito bites on her expressionless face and snot running down her forehead.

He was moving fast along the path and had soon left the crumbling buildings behind in a wake of hopeless sadness. It wasn't long before he found himself on the south end of the Old Asylum property with its neatly mown grass and rows of freshly built wooden crosses. This was the potter's field that inevitably accompanies any long-standing insane asylum and the sight of it brought Ambrose to a standstill. He knew only the cursory history of this funerary ground so was not privy to the many evil and despicable acts that had taken place on this land over the years. He knew nothing of the black masses performed amongst the crosses or the body pilfering that still sometimes takes place on the darkest, moonless nights. He knew nothing of these things, but Ambrose could sense that the potter's field was a bad place. Most everybody who wandered into this long forgotten corner of the county could tell as much. Even the usual potheads and weirdo kids that the police picked up from time to time for hanging out in the abandoned sections of the hospital shunned this flyblown field.

Standing on the edge of the woods overlooking the lawn, Ambrose remembered the way this field looked when he was a boy. The makeshift cemetery had been overgrown with briars and the decaying wooden crosses were so old that most of them had fallen over. It had been a forbidding and melancholy place back then and although it wasn't as spooky as it once was, the freshly planted grass and muddy machine tracks between the new crosses of pressure treated lumber seemed ominous in their own right. What had once been a semi-organized potter's field could now be more aptly described as a mass grave. Before the SIX SIX SIX plague hit, this burial site hadn't seen a funeral in over fifty years. Now with so many Book Club members filling the wards, the fallow earth was being put to regular use once more as the mortality rate of both hospitals steadily increased.

Ambrose stood there teetering on the edge of the woods, his grief threatening to bubble over completely. He glanced at the backhoe sitting silently on the edge of the field with its glossy yellow paint shining obscenely in the afternoon sun. Ambrose cringed, thinking that it should be painted black like a hearse. "Death and madness." He muttered, "How long before they use that machine to put Camilla in the ground? Camilla, Oh Camilla," he sobbed, "I love you Camilla." And then the full force of his grief broke through and he was on his knees in the dirt crying. His suit pants were getting filthy, his face was in the soil, but any sense of caring was behind him now. He thrashed and sobbed and broke down into the raw earth, convulsing onto his back like an infant having a tantrum. He had bottled his sadness for so long in order to be there for Camilla, but now in the leaves and the dirt it all flowed forth in hyperventilating tears.

Ambrose wept for his broken dreams until his throat was sore, his eyes were red, and his suit was a muddy ruin. As the crying jag began to pass, his racking sobs settled into feeble whimpers and he actually dozed off for a while in the underbrush at the edge of the Old Asylum cemetery. He slept there for some time until the third or fourth raindrop woke him with a start. It took a second for Ambrose to remember where he was and he groaned as his grief washed over him once more. Sitting up, he noticed that there was a sharp yellow tint to the sky and the air was thick with the ozone of an impending thunderstorm. As he wiped his eyes with the back of his tie and blew his nose onto the cuff of his shirt sleeve, the rain broke forth in a deluging torrent that instantly drenched him to the skin. Standing up a little too quickly he felt dizzy and weak, as if his extremities were made of gelatin and the rain was beating him back towards the ground. He wavered on his feet for a few seconds and briefly considered going back to finish his shift on T-Ward, but he just couldn't face her.

Despite the pounding rain he sought no shelter and didn't start back towards the Old Asylum like he knew he should. Instead he continued following *Sanitarium Road* on its winding path through the wooden crosses of the potter's field. He was moving at a much slower pace now that his anger and grief had been purged, but instead of gain-ing a sense of catharsis, Ambrose felt defeated and drained. Slogging through the downpour he began to talk to himself again. He had been doing that a lot lately. "Jesus Christ, what the hell happened? How did it get so bad? When the snot flew out of my nose and landed on her face she didn't even move. The old Camilla would have laughed out loud, or squealed in playful disgust, or maybe she would have gotten really pissed and punched me. At least she would have done something, god damn it, instead of just sitting there staring off into space all the time like some kind of zombie." This made him think back to the day of the tragedy and the stigmata she had gouged into her hands. Knitting was one of her hobbies and she liked to craft beanies and scarves while they watched TV in the evenings. "To keep my hands busy," she had said. When he found her in the closet, the stainless steel needles were stuck through her palms and she was jamming the spine of the *SIX SIX SIX* book up into the ruined crevice between her bloody legs.

It was just too much to think about and Ambrose's brain turned off as he trudged aimlessly through the rain. Soon he found himself at the wrought iron gate that opened into Sepulcher Hill, one of the largest private cemeteries in the state of New Jersey. This cemetery was so ancient that it predated the Old Asylum by nearly two centuries with burials going back to the early 1600's. The sagging fence marked the end of *Sanitarium Road* and also served as the border separating the Old Asylum's potter's field from the churchyard proper. The gate was an effective barrier for stopping cars, but it was open enough for Ambrose to easily slip through the gap and continue on with his aimless, trancelike walking.

Unlike the potter's field behind him, the headstones in Sepulcher Hill actually did mark the bodies they were supposed to represent. The deceased inhabitants of the ostentatious mausoleums and crypts had invested enormous amounts of money for the privilege of being interred on these hallowed grounds and their resting places were documented in stone. Sepulcher Hill was for paying customers only, not insane asylum indigents and Ambrose knew it fairly well because his own grandparents were buried somewhere in the more modern section, closer to the street.

As he shuffled aimlessly through the oldest section of the graveyard not even feeling the rain anymore, a sudden barrage of hailstones came whizzing down from the sky and began bashing him mercilessly in the head. The first few thumps on his skull effectively woke him from his grief and caused Ambrose to hastily run up the steps of the closest mausoleum in search of immediate shelter. The crypt he had inadvertently chosen was as large as a modest sized house, built entirely of black marble and topped with a pinnacle of onyx. He stood in the archway of the mausoleum, pressing backwards into the bronze doors as he tried to squeeze beneath the narrow overhang. All around him, the churchyard was experiencing a violent fusillade of ice raging down from the clouds and Ambrose was scared. On the grassy areas between headstones, the hail penetrated into the ground with deep thuds that reverberated across the cemetery. The hailstones that struck the grave markers and marble tops of the crypts shattered, spraying wide detonations of ice around each impact point. Ambrose pressed further back against the doors as he cowered from the wrath of the sky, but he was still partially exposed.

As the storm grew even fiercer in its intensity, a hailstone struck the lip of the marble arch and exploded directly into Ambrose's face. He recoiled from the ice bomb, jerking backwards in a violent spasm that accidentally knocked one of the mausoleum doors ajar. Out of necessity he stumbled backwards into the crypt and felt a sweet relief to be out of the furious storm, but this respite only lasted for a moment. Ambrose had never liked grave-yards and a wave of paralyzing fear clutched at his guts. In an agonizing display of will he swallowed his fear and forced himself to slowly turn around in order to peer into the depths of the tomb. It was an old mausoleum and the first thing he noticed was a collection of 7-day memorial candles flickering in their glass tubes atop a black marble altar. The date 1666 was etched onto the frontispiece of the slab and those numbers sent a chill up his spine. If it hadn't been for the whipping hail he would have turned around and ran from this tomb without ever looking back, but the stones fell from the sky in dark sheets and the ice was beginning to blanket the ground like a mid-summer snowstorm.

Leaving was impossible for the moment so instead Am-brose turned back to the altar and cautiously examined the inside of the mausoleum. He was in a spacious stone cham-ber and on either side of him were metal doors set into the marble. Each aperture was just the right size to receive a casket and Ambrose shuddered at the thought of the des-iccated corpses sleeping in their vaults. There were six of these catacombs on each side of the mausoleum and six cof-fin slots behind the black marble altar as well. Approaching the shrine with caution, Ambrose noticed that a hardcover book was open on the altar and the candles had been ar-ranged in a semi-circle to provide reading light. Looking closer at the open page, a lump rose in Ambrose's throat. He had seen this book before.

Most of the candles were burning low in their tubes and he would have had to squint to read the words there, but Ambrose didn't want to even look at the page. In a surge of anger he grabbed the book, snapped it shut, and slammed it facedown on the black altar. He hardly dared to look at the dread book, but almost involuntarily his eyes began to creep toward the forbidden object. He resisted with all his will, but before he knew it, his gaze was focusing on the author photo printed on the back cover. It was Hastur Chambers himself, a hideous looking man with hideous ideas turned poison on the page. As he stood there swaying in the candlelight, hypnotized by the author's eyes, Ambrose began to wonder what story *he* might find if he were to pick up the book and read those illicit words.

Ambrose hadn't seen that face since the day he pried the bloody hardcover from out of Camilla's hands as she defiled herself with it. Even then he had only caught a brief glimpse as he tossed it aside and called for help. The police had taken it with them as evidence, but he had seen that photo and Hastur's face was burned into his brain. Even in the midst of Camilla's climaxing madness Ambrose couldn't help himself from noticing those eyes. No sane person knew the true contents of the book before him and the people who had read it were reduced to howling psychotic shells, but still there was something tempting about *SIX SIX SIX* and Ambrose was feeling it now. Fresh tears welled in his eyes as he gazed upon Hastur Chambers' evil countenance. The man had stolen his happiness, destroyed his sweet Camilla and ruined the lives of so many others. He had died for his crimes; publicly hung in Washington Square Park, beheaded with a chainsaw and then torn to pieces by an angry mob, but it hadn't changed a thing. Ambrose had cheered along with the rest when he heard Chambers had been eradicated from the earth, but once the jubilation had faded he realized that no amount of vengeance would ever bring Camilla back.

It took some effort, but Ambrose broke the thrall of Hastur's stare and flipped the book over to examine the front cover, the words *SIX SIX SIX* were stacked on the page like an advancing army against an apocalyptic sky. For some reason it made him think of a piece of wisdom his boss had imparted on the first day of his job when Ambrose came to work at the Old Asylum. "These people in the *SIX SIX SIX* ward, or the 'Book Club' as we sometimes call it, are good people who tried to resist being corrupted." The doctor had told Ambrose, "They tried to fight against the book and it tore them apart. These inmates who you will be treating are the good people. They aren't the dangerous ones. The really terrifying people are the ones who were already evil to begin with. Those extremely rare types of bad people read this book and they don't freak out like normal folks do. They go mad all right, there's no disputing that, but instead of clawing their eyes out and stabbing stigmata in their hands they tend to go on massive killing sprees. Just look at that outbreak of *SIX SIX SIX* murders in upstate New York last week. The problem is that people like that embrace the evil in the book and no one even knows what's happening until they go berserk."

Ambrose pictured Camilla stoically resisting the *SIX SIX SIX* plague. He had once taken comfort from his boss's analysis, but now it broke his heart to think of Camilla fighting alone in the darkness behind her catatonic veil. In his mind's eye he saw her blank stare and the mosquitoes landing on her face. More tears splashed onto the black marble altar and he cried out, "Camilla, oh my god Camilla, I love you. If I read this book right now I will go insane, but if I do, then maybe by tonight I will be able to see what you're seeing and feel what you're feeling. I want to stand where you're standing and fight beside you. Camilla, I love you so much. If I read this book, maybe I will be able to find you in the darkness where you're lost." His hands were on the cover. Ambrose stood poised, ready to crack the spine. The hail fell outside from a yellow sky and tears coursed down his face. Whispering her name one last time, he opened the book.

Unlocked Cells of the Old Asylum

"A reporter from this news organization was briefly trapped earlier in the week when he ventured into a restricted area of the Old Asylum. He had permission from the county to be on the grounds, but had not been granted access to the interior of the abandoned mental hospital. Although he claims there was no wind at the time, he became locked on the female ward when a door mysteriously blew shut behind him. He was confined to the unit for approximately six hours until a sheriff's officer patrolling the grounds heard him beating on the door and investigated."

—2008 newspaper clipping from the author's collection

Welcome to Hell

"The nurses and orderlies are geniuses when it comes to inventing creative forms of torture. They seem to have a knack for figuring out the worst possible punishment to fit the individual. For me the restraint chair was the worst because I hate tight places and when you're in it you can't move a muscle not even your head. I used to act out a lot when I first came here, but they started strapping me to the chair and leaving me in a dark closet. Believe me it didn't take long before I changed my tune. I follow the rules now and I hope to get out soon."

—from an inmate letter dated 1983 found on the MICA ward

Blizzard Beast

We had been feeding a feral cat outside our house all winter that year. It was a particularly hard New Jersey winter with many significant snowfalls, weeks on end of frigid winds and long stretches of subfreezing temperatures. We had cats of our own so feeding the outside kitty seemed like the natural thing to do. We built a small heated shelter off the back of our garage for him to sleep and fed him at the same time of day that we gave food to our indoor cats. We called the outside cat Count Dracula because of his thick cloaklike mane of black hair and his piercing yellow eyes. He had become accustomed to the presence of my mother and I, but no matter how often we tried to tempt him with food, we couldn't lure him inside our warm home. We would have gladly matriculated him into the mix with our two middle-aged brown tabbies, but Dracula was feral to his bones. He tolerated our presence in the yard, but would not cross the threshold into the warmth, despite our frequent invitations.

Just as we began to let ourselves believe that the bad winter would soon be over, the Count abruptly disappeared. He was known to wander about the backyards of the neighborhood, but it had long become routine for him to show up at dawn for his breakfast and reappear every evening at dusk to eat his plate of food before hunkering down for the night. My mother was the first to notice his absence in the morning when she was preparing me a school lunch and serving breakfast, "Dracula didn't show up for his food this morning," she told me as she slid scrambled eggs onto my plate. At age eight, this news didn't register as an alarming fact the way it might now, having known a lifetime of pain and loss.

When mom picked me up from school that day she seemed distracted and melancholy. She was worried about the cat. When we got home she had me go upstairs and change into my snowsuit and then she helped me on with my wool hat, mittens and rubber snow boots. We stepped out the sliding glass doors onto our back deck, which was buried under several feet of drift. There was a thin path, only the width of a snow shovel leading to the stairs. Stepping off the deck onto the crust of the snow my mom's feet broke through, but I was light enough to walk right on top. Even with the approach of slightly warmer weather the backyard was a frozen, crystallized dreamland, dripping with ice facets that shimmered orange in the late afternoon sunlight. I shuffled lightly across the snow, instinctively distributing my weight so I wouldn't break through. My mother lagged behind in the deep drifts, hopelessly bogged down. "I'm not going to be able to get through this snow," she called. "You're going to have to look for the cat. Why don't you start over there at the fence? Try to get a look behind those bushes over there. See if you can find any sign of him."

I followed my mother's instructions, real concern starting to well inside me for Count Dracula. Amidst this concern was also a fear that behind those bushes, curled up in a ball, I might find the cat frozen stiff. Cautiously, I shuffled over to the bushes by the fence and peaked my head behind the icy leaves. To my relief there wasn't any animal there. After reporting this to my mother she instructed me to follow the perimeter of the fence, checking behind all the bushes and snowdrifts to see if there was any sign of him. Following the fence, I carefully examined every nook and cranny where an injured cat might hide, but didn't encounter anything. When I got closer to the house, not ten feet from where my mother was still standing up to her waist in snow, I used my gloved hand to push back a snow glazed pricker bush and suddenly called out in a prepubescent, high pitched scream, "I found him!"

My mother waded the distance through the high snow, plowing through the crust as it shattered in her wake. When she reached me I was still standing on the slippery ice rind, holding back the prickers so she could look in at the black, matted fur, half frozen into the crust. Seeing the body, which was still noticeably breathing, my mother let out a gasp. She started to bend over in order to pick up the cat, but at the last second seemed to hesitate. She withdrew a little bit and stood looking curiously at the wounded animal. I too was looking closely at the mass of fur laid out on the snow. There was something not quite right about the shape of the animal; something weird and unnatural about the way it was displayed on the snow. I asked my mom, "Is that the Count? I'm not quite sure it's a cat."

She didn't reply at first and just stood there, staring down at the animal with worry written across her face. When she did reply, it was without uncertainty, as if she had suddenly made up her mind. "Of course it's Dracula. Who else could it be? We have to get him inside." With that she bent down and began gently peeling the matted fur out of the ice. As she was pulling him from the crust I had a chance to look at the black wad of fur and was filled with a queasy, lightheaded feeling. As it became unstuck from the snow, a chill went up my spine that had nothing to do with the cold. I stood there in the bleak winter wind looking at my sad, graying mother holding the sick animal in her arms and couldn't help but ask her again, "Are you sure that's a cat?"

"Of course I'm sure," she snapped, "let's go inside." I stepped down off the ice crust and followed in her tracks as she moved through the snow trail that she had already broken, leading us back inside our warm house. We shook off our boots in the mudroom and she went directly into the downstairs bathroom instructing me to fetch some blankets and towels from the linen closet so she could make the cat comfortable and get him warmed up before taking him to the vet. I obediently ran upstairs and fetched the items, bringing them back downstairs and yelling to my mother that I had the towels ready. She called out, "He's just starting to wake up so I want to keep a firm grip on him. I'm going to open the door a crack and you can pass in the towels." With this, the door opened just wide enough for me to hand her the linens, promptly closing once the exchange was completed. Through the wooden door I could hear her arranging a makeshift cat bed with one hand while she spoke softly to the bundle in her arms.

At this point, my two indoor cats wandered over to the bathroom door and were standing at stiff attention with their tails fully puffed up, as if they sensed the presence of another animal in the house. I could hear my mother talking softly to the creature in her arms and then I heard another noise come through the door that sounded like a muffled roar, almost like the rumble of a lion on a nature show. My mother nervously exclaimed, "Oh my" and at the same moment the two indoor cats took off running in sheer terror. I heard my mother let out another gasp saying, "Oh my god!" I asked her what was going on in there and instead of a reply she let out a loud shriek.

Then the attack began. It didn't last long. The muffled roar I heard from inside the bathroom now became a hissing, screaming, raging howl mixed in with my mother's desperate pleas for god's mercy. I rattled the door, but my mother's weight must have been pressed against it because despite the terrible noises coming from within, I was unable to come to her aid. Inside the bathroom the sounds of struggle became even more violent, the door booming and crashing against its frame as my mother struggled inside with the crazed animal. Her agonized shrieking came to a frightful climax and then abruptly stopped as if she had been suddenly unplugged. I stood banging on the door with my small fist, crying and screaming myself sick. Inside the bathroom, the roaring and hissing had subsided and there presently came a distinct sucking and chewing sound.

I continued struggling with the door in a frantic attempt to get to my mother, but it was held tight from within. Finally after a prolonged period of nauseating lapping sounds I was able to partially push open the door. The instant the door began to swing inwards it was ripped from my hands and flung wide, toppling me forward into the tiny bathroom. I found myself face to face with a black, semi-humanoid beast of matted fur, perched atop my mother's eviscerated corpse. The thing was impossibly larger than a feral cat and considerably bigger than the lump of fur my mother had so innocently brought into our home. This was no cat at all. As it glared at me with iridescent yellow eyes, I became aware of its bloody mouth full of rapier teeth. I looked down at where its front legs should have been and saw the monster was equipped with glimmering five fingered claws protruding from tightly muscled forearms.

In an instant it was on me, tackling me to the ground and crushing me under its impossible weight. It seemed to be growing larger even as it pinned me to the floor. I felt its hot breath on my face as I cringed in panic with my eyes closed. Then, horror of horrors: I felt those terrible teeth bite into my face, the razor canines slicing through my eyelids and puncturing my delicate orbs. I was past screaming now as the beast began probing my face with its long tongue, lapping up the juice from the deflated eyeballs and sucking at the blood pouring from the wounds. I must have passed out around then because I awoke many months later in this hospital where I have been a ward of the state for the past thirty years.

The doctors and staff of this hospital say there was no black, matted beast. They say the black feral cat that my mother and I called Count Dracula never disappeared at all and that he was frequently seen about my old neighborhood for years until he eventually passed away. They say that at the age of eight years old I killed my beloved mother, ate her eyes, drank her blood and then ripped out my own eyeballs with my bare hands. Nonsense! The doctors and staff have told me many things, but I don't believe them and neither should you. There are monsters out there in the snow that will trick you into taking them inside. They use feral cat colonies to lure their prey, which are almost always compassionate mothers and their children. They love to taste human blood and have a particular hankering for innocent, young eyeballs that have not yet seen the horrors of life. I keep warning people about these Blizzard Beasts, but very few will listen, and of those who do take the time to hear my story; none believe.

That was the final day of my mother's life and the last time I would ever have the use of my vision. The very last image I retained into my brain was the black, matted demon sitting atop my mother's shredded corpse, her obscenely bloodied white skin crushed beneath the hairy weight of the beast. I see it before me now. I have told this story consistently without alteration of details since regaining consciousness thirty years ago, but no matter how convincing my tale may be it has done me no favors except to render me unfit to stand trial. My only comfort on this cold and lonely ward is the hospital's cat, which I have been told is all black with piercing yellow eyes. His name is Thomas, which I find to be absurd. Although the medical staff strictly forbids it, I secretly refer to the cat as Count Dracula. He comes to visit me often, especially when the weather gets cold. On those long frigid nights when I lay shivering in my bed, he creeps into my padded cell and curls up in the folds of my straightjacket to keep me warm. Despite the dangers, I still love cats.

Lonely Chair on the Crumbling Wards

"I visited the Old Asylum today in the rain. Instead of wandering the hallways or exploring the tunnels, I found a nice comfortable chair, cleaned it off, and sat quietly in the dayroom of the female ward. The hospital was alive with sounds. The rain pattered on the glass windows and dripped through the leaky roof. Gusts of wind blew through the empty hallways, repeatedly slamming the doors of the cells against their metal frames. I was at peace amongst the chaos of the abandoned hospital. During this meditation, a cop stopped at the window and peered in with cupped hands to the glass. I was sitting so still he didn't notice I was there."

—from the author's private notebook

The Trespasser

The Trespasser stood poised by the open window, ready to climb into the abandoned insane asylum. After a cautious hike through the forest and a quick dash across the road, he made it to the woods surrounding the building. Sweat poured from his face and adrenaline shook through his hands as he pointed his video camera into the basement and then hesitantly towards the group of uniformed officers huddled below in the parking lot. Having grown up in the area, the Trespasser knew these were the "almost cops," gung-ho rookies from the nearby police training academy. They often used the sanitarium gazebo for meetings, drills, and ceremonies. Their gathering was nothing unusual, but for the Trespasser it was cause for concern. Not being full-fledged 5-0, these recruits were on edge, salivating to make their first bust.

Above the squawk of the radios, the Trespasser could hear police dogs restlessly barking at their leashes in the hot August sun. The sound of the K-9s made him nervous, but he had made it this far and wasn't about to stop now. Judging by the shiny uniforms it didn't seem like the police planned to enter the building; they would have worn SWAT gear for that. It looked like they didn't want to get their uniforms dirty, but the Trespasser knew that if he was spotted by even one set of eyes, all fifty cadets would swarm into the Old Asylum and hunt him down like a fox.

On the wooded side of the Reception building he found a window that was open at the top. His camera rolled video as the Trespasser swung his leg over the bottom pane and climbed into the basement. The hospital smell hit him hard as his boots touched the floor. The insane asylum hadn't been abandoned long enough to lose its antiseptic stench. Second thoughts rushed through his mind, but the newspaper reported that demolition had already begun on the south end of the complex. The county's timetable for total destruction was less than six months away. This might be the Trespasser's last chance to see the portions of the Old Asylum he had not yet explored.

The room he entered was crammed with rusted shelves overflowing with moldy boxes of medical waste. The floor was crispy with peeled paint and fallen plaster. His steel toed boots crackled and echoed despite every attempt to remain quiet. When a squawk from a radio penetrated through the open window, the Trespasser was suddenly frozen in a wave of paranoia. Had the cops caught his scent? After a breathless pause, he swallowed his fear and quietly turned the knob leading into the basement corridor.

The hinges squeaked as he pulled the door towards him, collecting a large pile of paint chips and plaster dust on the floor as it swung. The darkness that lay beyond was thick and seemed to stream into the room, canceling out the small amount of light from the open window. He carried no flashlight, but felt a noticeable relief as he stepped into the blackness. It was nice to leave the police radios behind and surrender to the dark. Now, with rooms on both sides to mask the sound, he let his footfalls echo with less caution and began to explore the hallway by the intermittent flash of the camera.

The irregular bursts of light revealed crumbling walls lined with antique furniture and ancient medical devices. The Trespasser smiled in the darkness, happy to finally be experiencing this section of the Old Asylum. The wards in the main hospital buildings were some of the last abandoned. Now the patients were gone and decay reigned supreme.

The only landmark in the basement corridor was a thin crack of light surrounding a doorway. Swirls of rusty dust shimmered in the sunlight as the Trespasser parted the door from its frame with a dry squeak. X-ray equipment, bags of fluid, IV drips, and discarded hypodermic needles lined the shelves and floors. Raw medical waste was abundant in this basement laboratory. The Trespasser's camera greedily clicked away at the hospital files and patient records that had been left behind.

Rummaging through the filth, he came across a stack of X-ray slides and a set of trays used for developing the images. There was one box that lay open on the table. The Trespasser switched his camera to movie mode and used his bare hand to close the slide. It wasn't until later, when reviewing the footage, that he realized he had foolishly exposed himself to radiation. The crackling and spitting of the invisible particles were clearly captured as interference on the video. Later, while watching the footage at home, it occurred to the Trespasser that the thick rubber gloves and lead-lined aprons had probably been hanging on the wall for good reason.

Next to the X-Ray room, there was a sterilization center that had once served the entire hospital. The medical waste was thick and moldy in this room, piled high atop hospital gurneys and strewn about on the floor. As the Trespasser stepped lightly through this hazardous filth, industrial-sized sterilization chambers gave way to strange chemistry sets complete with glass distillation jars, pressure gauges and rotting rubber tubes. At the far end of the sterilization room, a doorway led him into a damp corridor where he was greeted by a warm wind steadily blowing from the entrance of an underground tunnel.

The Trespasser was familiar with these tunnels from his own illegal explorations and from a very special tour he had received as a kid. In his youth, he had briefly held a position at a public relations agency, one of his many failed attempts at keeping a job. This PR firm happened to represent the local union in charge of operating the boilers at the Old Asylum. One of his early writing assignments was to go to the sanitarium and interview the engineers for the union newsletter. These interviews were an opportunity for the Trespasser to see the underbelly of the still-working complex. It provided a sanctioned occasion to photograph and explore the steam tunnels and even came with a guided tour. The engineer who showed him around was more than happy to allow the Trespasser into his subterranean world. They walked what seemed like miles of tunnel, ducking steam pipes and avoiding cave crickets. The tunnels connected the buildings and one by one they stopped at steel doors to peer through reinforced-glass windows into the basements of the locked wards.

Now, standing at the entrance, looking into the blackness of the tunnel, it didn't seem as inviting as on the Trespasser's guided tour. The lights had been on back then when the tunnels were in use. Now, the darkness was inky and thick. The damp air flowing ceaselessly across his face spoke of asbestos, crickets, and dripping water. The warm draft also suggested a current of life that still breathed beneath the abandoned hospital and served as a foul, rotting jet stream for the ghosts. Without a flashlight, the tunnels were too forbidding. After snapping a couple pictures of this dark aperture, the Trespasser turned around and resumed his search for the stairs.

When he finally found the door, he was nearly blinded by the sunlight shining into the stairwell. Paint peeled like a bad case of poison ivy, bubbling up the walls and oozing dust. The air was dead and stale, reeking of old hospital. Sweat ran down the Trespasser's body, but his muscles felt strong and alive, pulsing with the Old Asylum's phantom heartbeat. Climbing the stairs, the Trespasser ignored the lower wards and headed directly to the top floor. Turning the corner into the hallway, he found himself in the dentistry wing. Vintage dental chairs sat abandoned under thick layers of dust. Shelves and workstations overflowed with discarded dentist tools and unused prescription drugs. The Trespasser spent a considerable amount of time in these rooms, going through each and every drawer and cataloging the contents with his camera.

There was nothing of value because many an explorer had been through here already, but the apparatus made for some nice photographs. All that was left were antibiotics, outdated Novocain, rusting scalpels, and moldering denture making supplies, but they formed quite a still life for the lens. After thoroughly going through the exam rooms, the Trespasser made his way into the waiting area, which was covered in spray paint and medical trash. In the middle of the room was an 8mm projector with reels of film strewn about its base. The Trespasser was especially interested in the film and held it up to the windows to try and see the images. As he crouched on the floor, examining the reel, a bright red patch on the tiles caught his attention. Forgetting the film, which was crudely shot and blurry anyway, he made his way toward the red goo. At first it looked like someone had spilled a red slushy, but as the Trespasser got closer, the goo took on more of a gelatin texture, as if a giant gummy worm had melted in the sun.

Something about this mysterious slime repulsed the Trespasser. That, coupled with the radio squawks that were still coming through the windows, made him want to branch out into the other sections of the building that weren't so close to the police gathering. Back in the hallways, it didn't take long to locate the corridor bridging the hospital complex together. The Trespasser had driven under this bridge many times when the Old Asylum was still in operation, yearning for the time when the buildings would be abandoned. He couldn't see it, but a huge smile was written across his face as he peered down the long hallway. He was finally fulfilling the lifelong goal of seeing the main wards from the inside.

He crept through the hall, pointing his camera out the windows, capturing the grand scale of the hospital from the inside out. Somehow this one corridor perfectly personified the Old Asylum and captured the mood of the anguish, suffering and death that once took place here. The sanitarium had opened in the late 1800s and, back then, their methods of treating the insane leaned more towards torture than therapy. Frankenstein-style laboratories, electric shock treatments, medieval restraint practices and a general ignorance about the nature of mental illness made the Old Asylum a particularly bad place to be a crazy person.

Thousands were tortured within these walls under the

guise of medical treatment and this hallway captured the mood. In his mind, the Trespasser imagined patients wandering in their gowns and lining up at prescribed times to receive their medications. He could almost see the schizos, psychos, murderers and suicide attempts aimlessly shuffling through the peeling paint. The Trespasser had read many histories and archived news articles about the Old Asylum and was aware of the wretched conditions that existed here for the patients. The summers were sweltering in the locked wards with nothing but fans to blow around the stagnant reeking air. The winters were drafty and, because of the steam heating, the wards closest to the boilers would be sopping with heat while the furthest would get so cold that a layer of ice sometimes formed in the toilets.

There was a winter here in the early 1930s when the boilers broke down and could not be immediately fixed. During the ensuing month, twenty seven patients froze to death, with many more suffering from severe frostbite. This was the Old Asylum's most publicized tragedy. The 4-drawer morgue was pushed far beyond its capacity, forcing the newspapers and politicians to take notice of a problem they would just as soon brush under the rug. Mental illness isn't pretty, which is why the Old Asylum was setup more like a prison than a hospital. It was a place to lock away society's undesirables so as not to embarrass family and friends. The sealed wards were built to cage the madness so it couldn't get out into the general public and the majority of the Old Asylum's occupants were unaccounted for and unloved.

The Trespasser could feel the ghosts of the abandoned sanitarium on the hot drafts of air flowing through the decaying hallways. Pain was evident here; from the hospital smell, to the ancient equipment, to the empty chairs still inhabited by the spirit of insanity. There had been much death within these wards and much suffering. The peeling walls, the stagnant heat, the festering shadows all retained the mood of trauma. Yet despite this legacy of madness, the Trespasser felt at home here. What is it about these buildings that have always called to him? What attracts the Trespasser to the darkness and the soiled history of the Old Asylum?

Perhaps it was his own internship in the Mentally Ill Chemically Addicted unit that cemented his love for these buildings. Although the Trespasser was never a patient in the hospital, he had been, in his adolescence, a trustee. He had been given the key to the MICA Ward and it was his job to make coffee for the twelve-step meeting, which met every Friday at 11:00 PM.

The meeting was called Late Night. It was aimed at attracting young people who were freshly clean. Originally the group met in a church basement, but due to the age bracket of the attendees it tended to be a rowdy crowd and eventually they were kicked out. A few devoted members, the Trespasser included, did not want the meeting to die. Luckily it turned out that some people knew some people and, after strings were pulled, Late Night found a new home at the MICA unit of the Old Asylum.

At the time, the Trespasser wasn't necessarily staying clean by choice. It was a forced sobriety, but once Late Night moved to the Old Asylum, he embraced this particular meeting. He volunteered to make coffee for the group, which meant he was given a key and was expected to show up early to set up the meeting. On Fridays, he would arrive two, sometimes three hours ahead of schedule just so he could wander the ward. These were the days when the hospital was still in operation, but on Friday nights the entire MICA unit was empty. At first he was alone in these pre-meeting hours, but as the weeks rolled by, his friends started showing up early as well. It didn't take long for the Back Male Hill and the adjacent MICA ward to become the Trespasser's own personal clubhouse where one could always find the cute girls fresh out of rehab and the young junkies come to collect their sobriety fix.

As usual, the meeting often got loud and out of hand, but this time there was no one to complain. Most Fridays the addicts would stay long past the serenity prayer; talking, guzzling coffee, and gobbling cigarettes as if they were candy. It was during these times, when the lights were turned down and the long corridors were lit only by the exit signs, that the Trespasser would strap on an old pair of roller skates from the games closet and glide through the hallways. One night, he found a steel medical cart with a good set of wheels that made for an excellent impromptu rickshaw. One of the girls at the meeting eagerly hopped aboard and the Trespasser rolled her around for hours, skating over the smooth tile floors of the Old Asylum like an outboard motor pushing a boat.

As the fun evolved, the meeting began to grow. It had always been candle lit at the church, but in the MICA dayroom the darkness ate the light from the few measly candles the group could afford. Using his own money, the Trespasser fixed this problem by embarking on a frenzied candle-collecting spree. He raided every thrift shop, Salvation Army, garage sale, and dollar store. The result was a pyre of candles set up on an altar in the middle of the Back Male Ward. Every Friday night, young addicts sat around this small inferno and poured their hearts out to the group. Perhaps it was the hypnotic flicker of the candles that opened people up, or maybe it was the mood of the sanitarium itself, but whatever the cause, the secrets came pouring out of people. Shocking revelations were made, teary confessions were heard and a certain safety was achieved for a bunch of lost kids in an otherwise insane world.

So is this why the Trespasser feels safe here? Is this why he feels he has the right to walk these halls even though there are fifty wannabe cops just below who would arrest him on sight? Is it arrogance or proprietorship that allows the Trespasser to wander these abandoned corridors unobstructed by ghost or man?

None of these questions mattered as he crept low through the buildings. His only thought was to see as many of the wards as possible before the afternoon sun went behind the mountain. He made his way through the wings of the Old Asylum with a silence and purpose long practiced on the outskirts of the hospital. Along the way, he diligently captured photos and video for he knew these walls wouldn't stand for much longer. When the heat and smell had finally taken its toll, and the longing for a drink of cold water had become overpowering, he snuck out of the hospital and managed to get back to his vehicle without being seen. As he drove home, the adrenaline was still pumping through his veins, but even as he congratulated himself on a job well done, he knew his mission wasn't fully accomplished. There was still one room he could not rest without seeing: the morgue.

For weeks it bothered the Trespasser that he had not found the morgue. He had sworn to himself not to risk another trip to the hospital, but it gnawed at him. He even began to dream about it. Meanwhile, the police presence was intensifying. Newspapers published stories almost daily about the arrests of curious thrill seekers on the

Old Asylum property. It turned out that the same day the Trespasser was there, six people had been arrested on the hospital grounds for trying to break in. Those arrests capped a month long crackdown, which netted over forty tickets for criminal trespass. The Trespasser knew the risks perhaps better than anyone, but like a bird watcher after an endangered species; he had to see the morgue for his life list.

He woke one morning to the sounds of a rumbling August thunderstorm and decided today would be the day. On his last visit to the Old Asylum, the path to the building had been much too crackly. He had been waiting for rain to soften the leaves of the forest floor and finally it had arrived. Over his morning coffee, the Trespasser reviewed once more the online satellite images of the Old Asylum property. He would follow the same plan as before; park in the lot at the end of Lewis Drive, duck into the woods and follow the trail up the hill. Halfway up the mountain he would sneak across the athletic field, ducking under the hill so motorists couldn't see him from Sanitarium Road. From space, he could see the small clump of bushes where he would catch his breath. Then, making sure no one was coming, he would dash across the road and almost instantly be in the patch of trees behind the Front Male Hill. From there he would make his entrance through the same open window of the Reception Wing he had used on his previous visit.

This route had worked perfectly last time and the Trespasser saw no reason to deviate. As he sipped his morning coffee he watched some online videos which he knew contained footage of the morgue. It was hard to discern many clues as to where it would be, but the Trespasser had a good feeling that it would be in the basement of the Reception building, which was the lowest, darkest vault in the Old Asylum.

He parked, hiked, scrambled, huffed, puffed, and all went well until he was about a hundred yards from the building. The Trespasser was walking through the second set of woods with his sights on the open window when he heard the engine of a car suddenly come around the corner. He had been creeping through the wet leaves on the slope of the hill to avoid being spotted from above, but was dangerously exposed to the parking lot below. Acting quickly, the Trespasser dropped into the dirt behind a tree and lay motionless on the edge of the forest. His fetal form was only partially concealed and he prayed that his camouflage clothing would be enough to hide him in plain sight. Through squinting eyes, he watched the police car round the corner and come to an idling stop fifteen feet below him in the parking lot. Waves of paranoia rushed through the Trespasser and he was sure that this time he had been caught. But after a few minutes gabbing on a cell phone the officer once again resumed his patrol.

The Trespasser stood with shaky knees and hobbled towards the building. With exquisite care he swung his leg over the windowpane and climbed quietly into the basement. Sweat poured from his face and his hands shook. Once again he was unaware of it, but there as a smile written across his face. Quietly he tiptoed through the file room and eased the door open into the basement corridor. He made his way slowly through the blackness on tiptoe, unwilling to give up any sounds that would betray his presence. It was slow going down the hall and he stopped to examine the rooms along the way to make sure he didn't miss the morgue.

Halfway down the corridor the Trespasser heard the

police driving slowly through the complex and looked out a basement window just in time to see the tires roll past. He froze in the hallway, heart beating, breath catching, paranoid, hunted, scared. For almost a minute he could neither move forward or back, but could only stand in the dark like a statue. He found himself wishing that he could just be somewhere else, some place nice where there were no cops and no darkness and no ghosts.

Finally though, he found his balls and crept once more towards where he was sure the morgue was to be found. In these matters the Trespasser's instincts are seldom wrong. The morgue was indeed located at the end of the hall and as he peeked through the last door on his right, his ambitions were rewarded. He wasted no time taking pictures of his prize and it's a good thing, because his camera only clicked 5 times before the police once again pulled up. This time, instead of rolling past the car stopped almost directly outside. The cruiser continued to idle while two car doors slammed and all of a sudden there were footsteps and talking from outside. The Trespasser didn't dare to even breathe and instinctively crouched into a corner of the tiled morgue. Spider webs enveloped him as he pressed himself into the corner and he felt something crawling on the back of his neck, but couldn't afford to make even the slightest of sounds. The voices were getting closer, echoing through the basement hallway.

The Trespasser knew he was caught. He knew that these police would enter the building. He knew they would want to see the morgue. He knew they would find him and he knew he would be arrested. He knew these things and suddenly with knowledge came acceptance. The fear vanished and the smile returned to his face. What could the cops really do anyway? The Trespasser could afford the fine. Would they rough him up a bit? The Trespasser isn't afraid to take a punch. When it came down to an actual confrontation the Trespasser found himself strangely relieved and unafraid. It might have been this sudden drainage of panic that stopped the cops from entering the building. Like any predator, police are drawn to the smell of fear. The Trespasser's sudden calm must have thrown them off the scent. He heard the cops walk up the outside stairs, get back in the car and slowly drive away.

Once they were gone the Trespasser stood up, brushed the spider webs from the back of his neck and tiptoed out of the room. His fear was gone, but he wasn't stupid. It was time to get the hell out of these buildings at least for today. Scampering down the long hallway, the Trespasser was soon out the window and into the woods. He padded lightly through the small copse of trees and caught one last glimpse of the patrol car as it exited the Old Asylum grounds. Five pictures of the morgue were tucked safely in the memory card of his digital camera. The Trespasser was happy.

Demolition Open Attic PEER Building

"When they started to tear down the buildings I visited the Old Asylum on a daily basis to document the process. On more than one occasion, I was actually inside while the wrecking machines were tearing away at the facade. Yesterday I was up in the attic of the PEER building while the machines tore off the face of the structure. It was incredibly loud and probably extremely dangerous, but there was a certain catharsis about inhabiting my old haunt while they actively demolished the building around me. I went back today and the entire PEER facility is gone, reduced to a pile of rubble."

—from the author's private notebook

Basement Hallway Tunnel Entrance

"The whole asylum is connected by underground tunnels so they can heat the place with steam pipes. There is a woman patient on the female ward (I won't mention her name) and she passed me a note telling me how to meet up using the tunnel system. I'll admit she isn't much to look at, but when you're in here you learn to take what you can get. I managed to sneak down and meet her during the night and let's just say she taught me a thing or two down there in the dark. Crazy girls aren't exactly wife material, but if you ever get the chance to take one for a ride I advise that you seize the opportunity."

—from an undated letter found in a folder marked: Confiscated

The Dry Man

ntil his mid-twenties, the one who was to become known as the *Dry Man*, hadn't had much experience with body lotion, lip moisturizer or any other beauty products. For many years, his only toiletries consisted of a bar of soap, a can of shaving cream and a disposable razor. He kept his hair clipped short, didn't wear jewelry and always dressed in muted tones. Perhaps it was this simplicity and lack of attention to his personal appearance that kept him single for so long. When he finally did manage to attract a member of the opposite sex, it was she who turned him on to the pleasures and benefits of well-hydrated skin.

At first he did benefit. His skin had never felt so sleek and alive as when he slathered his entire body in cocoa butter. After toweling off from his nightly shower he would rub himself with lotion and not need another application for at least twenty-four hours. When he leaned back on his computer chair at work his back didn't itch anymore, and when he removed his dress shoes at the end of the day there were no longer snow banks of skin flakes covering his socks. He began applying lip balm throughout the day as well and it had never felt so smooth or natural just to simply smile.

His girlfriend noticed these changes and began to enjoy his touch, which was no longer papery and dry. True, his newfound hygiene wasn't enough to keep her exclusive, after all she was young and free, but what he learned from her had helped him to be more comfortable in his own skin, and for that he was grateful. She couldn't offer him a committed relationship, but she had given him the gift of hydration so he didn't begrudge her when she inevitably moved on. Over the years there were a few hopeful starts with various other ladies, but none of these trysts amounted to much of anything and he eventually resigned himself to being alone.

By his mid-thirties, the Dry Man had acclimated fairly well to a solo lifestyle, but all the while he was progressively increasing his moisturizing habits to an unhealthy degree. He lived alone in a small apartment with no pets. He kept his refrigerator sparsely stocked with TV dinners and other prepackaged, simple to prepare meals. He awoke on time every day from an untroubled sleep, slathered on his ritualistic cocoa butter, applied his lip balm, dressed in his conservative suits and put in eight hours at his cubicle. In the evening he would come home from work, prepare himself a quick meal, take a shower, towel off and then apply a liberal amount of cocoa butter to his entire body. From head to toe he would work the lotion into his skin until all of it had absorbed and then he would swab several layers of balm onto his lips and the areas around his mouth.

Once properly hydrated, he could finally relax, but before sitting down to watch his shows, his ritual demanded that he take the time to set up what he called his *hydration station*. This moisturizing tableau consisted of a one-liter bottle of orange flavored seltzer, a tube of raspberry lip balm, and thirty-two ounce container of cocoa butter. From the seltzer he would take frequent sips and whenever his skin felt dry, he would pour a dollop of lotion onto his hands to properly lubricate. In the early years of this routine he had only moderately moisturized, but over time he had progressed to the point where he was applying the lip balm after every sip of seltzer, and lubing his hands with cocoa butter every five minutes or so. Maybe if he had found a partner there would have been someone to caution him from indulging so freely in this hydration obsession, but love wasn't in the stars for the Dry Man and his nights remained his own.

One would think that after so many applications of cocoa butter his skin would be left feeling oily and wet, but the actual results were quite to the contrary. It seemed the more lotion and lip balm he applied, the faster his thirsty skin would drink it up. It got to the point where he carried lotion with him everywhere he went, including work. Throughout the day he would take several bathroom breaks, locking himself into a stall and smearing cocoa butter on his back, trying to cover as much skin as he could without removing his shirt and tie. These eccentricities did not go unnoticed by his fellow employees, who always whispered amongst themselves whenever they saw him taking the lotion bottle into the bathroom.

Eventually, his coworkers came to accept these daily forays to the bathroom and ended up tolerating them for years, even as their frequency increased. Early on, the matter had been investigated and it was deduced that he was in fact only applying lotion to his body and not doing anything nefarious or sexual. This deduction was accomplished by a small troupe of giggling male office workers sent in as spies to ascertain exactly what was happening in the bathroom. By taking turns peeking through the gaps in the stall, they were able to catch glimpses of the Dry Man struggling to reach up under his shirt in order to cover every inch of his back with cocoa butter. Then they saw him pull up his pant legs as high as they would go so he could rub lotion over his calf muscles and hydrate behind his knees. They reported their findings to the rest of the office, confirming that he was only rubbing lotion on his skin and not doing anything sexual, prompting one woman to say, "His skin must be exceptionally dry if he needs to use that much lotion. We should call him the Dry Man."

Of course, the name stuck.

The Dry Man's hydration obsession was beginning to cause minor disturbances in his life, but despite his ever-increasing trips to the lavatory he was still able to get his work done in a timely fashion, so his coworkers allowed themselves to get used to his eccentricities. In the parlance of addiction his life was still *manageable*, but as you can guess this perilous equilibrium between hydration and sanity was quickly tipping towards uncontrollable lubrication.

In his thirty-ninth year, his need for hydration finally cost him his job. He had been taking lotion breaks a little too often lately and when he was discovered fully disrobed in the bathroom stall on his lunch hour, applying cocoa butter to every part of his body, it was simply too much for management to forgive. His actions having finally been brought to light, the Dry Man was forced to explain to his supervisors that his act was not one of sexual perversion, but an unfortunate case of an extremely dry epidermis that required almost constant hydration. He begged his bosses not to terminate him and tried to make them understand that if this hydration was not applied on an hourly basis it would cause him to practically writhe in his own skin. His bosses were not appeased by this information and he was promptly fired without severance pay. He left that day a broken man, realizing that he had a serious problem and wondering what he was going to do to support himself.

On the way home, still shaking from the confrontation, these anxieties led him to do something he had never done before; stop in at the liquor store and buy himself a bottle of strong drink. He wasn't sure what kind to get and he eventually settled on a pint of vodka because it was clear and didn't look as menacing as the brown liquors. He wasn't much of a drinker, perhaps taking a glass of wine on special occasions or enjoying a microbrew at the company holiday party, but tonight he was feeling down and needed something strong. Before going back to his apartment, he also turned in at the drugstore and bought two fresh bottles of cocoa butter along with two tubes of raspberry lip balm. This exchange drew smirks from the teenagers behind the counter who were familiar with his purchases and assumed he was using the lotion for other purposes besides hydration.

Locking the door to his apartment, the Dry Man could feel his itching, flaking skin, which hadn't been freshly lotioned since being caught several hours ago in the bathroom at work. The safe period between applications of cocoa butter had long since elapsed and he was frantic to rehydrate. Ripping off his suit and throwing the crumpled dress shirt into a pile on the otherwise neat floor, the Dry Man cracked open one of the cocoa butter bottles, unscrewed the pump top and dumped a quarter of the contents directly on his head. He then took his hands and began rubbing the sloppy beige lotion onto his entire expanse of skin, luxuriating in the healing hydration as his flaking crust was appeased with its necessary chemicals. His body was so dry from the time between applications, that he was forced to slosh more of the cocoa butter out onto his hands so he could continuously apply it to his back, struggling to rub lotion into every pore.

Having performed this lubrication ritual to excess and after numerous applications of raspberry lip balm, the Dry Man finally began to feel like himself again. As he stood naked in the middle of his small apartment, he closed his eyes and searched his entire body with his mind's eye, seeking any dry spots he might have missed. Finding none, he opened his eyes and began putting on his pajamas. Once he was dressed and comfortable, he lined up his seltzer, the now half empty cocoa butter container and the bottle of vodka he had purchased. Clicking on the TV, he turned the volume low so he could just barely hear it and then set about applying another coat of lotion to his hands and face, which had partially dried out while he was settling in. Feeling hydrated again, he sat back on his couch and reached for the vodka bottle. Cracking the seal on the plastic cap, he tentatively smelled the liquid inside. It reeked of medical disinfectant and he tried to think back, wondering if he had ever tried this type of alcohol before.

Taking a sip from the pint bottle he almost regurgitated at the strength of the vodka, but managed to choke it down. The liquid fire burned through his hydration, prompting him to uncap his lip balm and apply it liberally around his mouth to combat the heat from the alcohol. "Yuck," he bitterly exclaimed, setting the bottle down and reaching for the cocoa butter. After applying another coat of lotion on his hands, lower back and elbows he began thinking about the job he had lost today. Most people finding themselves newly unemployed would be scared to lose their house, their car, or the clothes off their back, but not the Dry Man. He voiced his fears aloud to the TV.

"What if I can't afford cocoa butter? My god I'll dry up if that happens." With these thoughts he turned again to the bottle. The slight sip he had taken was warming him from the inside, and although it had been unpleasant to choke down, he needed escape so badly that he was willing to overcome his dislike of alcohol just for the oblivion he knew it could offer.

In one crazy swipe he took the pint bottle off the table, unscrewed the cap and poured the contents down his throat. It didn't burn as bad when chugging it like this so he didn't stop until the entire bottle was empty. Then it did burn and badly, but within a matter of minutes he was too insensible to register the fire in his belly. Never in his life had the Dry Man taken in this much alcohol and it caused him to pass out, his tongue lolling out of his mouth as he slumped over on the couch.

Fifteen minutes later, in a state of extremely groggy drunkenness, he was awakened from his stupor by the incessant needling of the telephone ringing on its cradle by the side of the couch. His coordination was failing him, but out of habit he reached for the phone, knocking it off the hook by way of answering it. It took some time for his fumbling drunken hands to find the receiver, but once he got it to his ear, he managed to greet the other person on the line without slurring, "Hello?"

"Hi this is Sharon from the office, how are you? I just wanted to say that I'm so sorry you got fired today. How are you holding up?"

Sharon was a middle-aged, divorced mother of two, who sat across the room from his cubicle. She was one of the few people in the office who didn't refer to him as the *Dry Man*. She had been watching him for almost two years, thinking he was eccentric and weird, but kind of cute in a plain, harmless sort of way. With the encouragement of her non-work friends, she had been recently building up her courage to talk to him on a more intimate level, but had waited too long and was now reaching out by telephone as a last resort. "Are you OK?" She asked, "I feel really bad about what happened to you."

The Dry Man, who was usually so tongue-tied around women and who had all but given up on love, suddenly perked up from his drunkenness and sat up on the couch. Switching the phone to speaker-mode so he could apply more cocoa butter to his hands and body, he began a rambling explanation of why he had to use lotion on his skin at least every hour. By talking very fast he found that he could keep his slurring to a minimum and, as the conversation progressed he was reasonably sure that Sharon had no idea that he had just guzzled a pint of vodka, or had been drinking at all.

On the other end of the phone, Sharon was taking in this explanation of why he had to apply so much lotion with a quiet acceptance. She was fully aware of the reason why he had been fired, as was everyone in the office, and she was well acquainted with the Dry Man's frequent bathroom breaks. It was hard not to notice when he would return from the lavatory smelling strongly of drug store fragrances, and have unabsorbed lotion streaks in his hair with cocoa butter stains spotting his suit. Sharon was a compassionate woman who had some slight OCD issues of her own, so she was able to empathize and look past the Dry Man's strange proclivities. After hearing his chaotic, explosive explanation, which she naively attributed to emotion rather than alcohol, she sympathized even further with the Dry Man and asked him if he would like to come over to her house for a nice home cooked meal. "Also, you can bring all the cocoa butter you need if it will make you more comfortable. I have some brand-name skin lotion here if you need it, but something tells me I probably don't have enough to keep you happy."

The Dry Man considered her offer through the haze of vodka clouding his brain. He had secretly snuck glances in Sharon's direction and her small attempts at flirtation had not gone unnoticed by him; although at the time he had always been too shy or too preoccupied with hydration to reciprocate. The vodka was giving him confidence, however, and although a small voice in the back of his head was telling him that it was a bad idea, he found himself agreeing to meet Sharon for a nice home-cooked meal at her house just across town.

After hanging up the phone, the Dry Man drunkenly removed his pajamas and repeated his full hydration ritual, dumping out cocoa butter onto the top of his head and then slathering the lotion over every inch of his body. When it had absorbed into his skin enough where he felt well lubricated, he commenced gathering his suit off the floor and clumsily put it back on. If he hadn't been drunk, he never would have put on his crumpled suit and probably never would have agreed to go to Sharon's house at all. But as he struggled with his shoelaces, the drink in him gave a false confidence that propelled him blunderingly forward. Grabbing the keys off the hook by the door, he stepped out into the hallway and promptly blacked out. Staggering down the hall, leaving his apartment door wide open, the Dry Man had no clue what he was about to get himself into.

He awoke the next morning on a hard bench in a small concrete jail cell wearing an orange jumpsuit. Looking around, he struggled to make sense of where he was. Reaching back into his memories from last night, he could find no explanation as to why he was waking up in prison. The holding cell where he was confined was a very small single occupancy with painted cinderblock walls, a toilet/sink combination, a solid metal door with a thick glass observation window and a food slot that was currently locked in the closed position. The Dry Man sat up with a groan and put his papery hand to his throbbing head. "What happened?" He muttered aloud, but before he could think too much about why he was locked up, the fear hit him. "What if I can't get cocoa butter in here?" His hands went up to his cracked lips, "what if I can't get my lip balm?"

Just then a rattling of keys could be heard outside the cell and the food tray slot opened with a jarring slam. A pair of cruel brown eyes looked in at the huddled Dry Man on the bench. "Breakfast burrito?" The guard quipped as he slid a plastic tray containing different compartments of unappetizing mush through the slot. "You're gonna love the food here Drunky! A-one, first-class cuisine."

The Dry Man rushed at the door causing the guard to instinctively flinch back away from the food slot. Placing the tray on the ground he implored the officer to tell him how he had ended up in this jail cell. The guard gladly imparted the Dry Man's infraction with a righteous, sadistic glee. "You're a drunk. You were driving. Want to guess how many people you ran over? With blood alcohol like yours, it's a miracle that you didn't kill yourself as well. Sorry Drunky, but it looks like you are going to be here a long time. And guess what, drinks aren't on the menu. No booze allowed!"

"Please sir, please. I am sorry! Please, can you bring me some hand lotion or lip balm? I have a very rare condition and I must hydrate my skin."

The guard chuckled softly and put his face closer to the slot. "Sorry Buddy, but you're going to have to get used to not getting what you want in here. That's just the way it goes...." With that, the food slot slammed shut and the chuckling guard sauntered down the hall. In his cell, the Dry Man withered to the floor and went insensible once more, passing out into oblivion.

The first thing he felt upon waking was an incredible thirst and he fumbled about for the usual bottle of seltzer he always kept by the bed. Instead of a cool, bubbling seltzer his fingers blundered into the pile of coagulating gruel on his food tray. Flinching from the detestable mush, he began groping along the floor but soon recoiled from the dry concrete as it sought to rob his hands of whatever precious moisture they still contained. He brought those dry husks up to his face and felt around his mouth where he encountered coagulated blood and shriveled skin around his badly desiccating lips. His tongue felt like sandpaper on the roof of his mouth and his back was tortured by a stale, restless itch that couldn't be scratched away. His worst fear was coming true. He was drying out.

Pulling himself upright with a tremendous effort, the Dry Man made an attempt to take a drink from the metal sink, but could only choke down a few sips. His throat was so incredibly parched that it felt like the skin of his esophagus was peeling away. Splashing water from the sink onto his arid, flaking body, his peeling skin absorbed the moisture like a sponge, but was almost immediately dry by the time he sat down on the hard jail cell bench. What the Dry Man did not realize was that he was long past the point where he could rehydrate with mere water. Without his daily dose of theobroma cacao, lanolin, mineral oil, sodium lauryl sulfate, propylene glycol, benzyl benzoate and methylparaben, the key ingredients of his beloved cocoa butter, he was going to stay dry and become dryer still.

As he sat on the bench, head in hands, a restless agony crept over his body. He could feel every inch of his skin evaporating and cracking like a low-tide mud flat on a hot summer day. Looking down at his arms, he saw that where he had doused his skin with water, the drying effect was especially predominant, causing the top layers of his skin to slough off in thick parchment sheets. In a fit of desperation, the Dry Man cast off his jumpsuit and fell back to the floor. He crawled to the food tray and began scooping up globs of the putrid jail food, applying it to his face in an attempt to treat his rapidly crumbling epidermis. The breakfast on the tray consisted of a yellow slush somewhat resembling scrambled eggs, a portion of runny black beans, something that looked like oatmeal and a crust of stale bread. Wiping the eggs and oatmeal on his face brought a small modicum of relief and the beans smeared on his back brought a momentary reprieve from the maddening chalky itch, but his discomfort soon returned in spades as the food lost its moisture. His skin had reached such an advanced state of desiccation that it rapidly absorbed whatever greasy hydration the jail food had to offer, leaving behind a scab-like layer of thick-crusted food that covered most of his body.

As the Dry Man lay squirming and naked on the dusty floor, the food slot was suddenly opened with a bang and the same sadistic guard peeked in, his disembodied voice requesting the tray back. When he saw the Dry Man flopping in agony on the floor covered in the remains of his breakfast, he let out a chuckle and then spoke mockingly through the slot, "Looks like you're having fun in there. Decided to wear your breakfast instead of eating it I see, interesting fashion choice Buddy. The nut jobs on the twelfth floor are going to love you. You're going to feel right at home up there with the rest of the lunatics. Pass me that food tray."

The Dry Man writhed on the floor, his skin beginning to peel back in earnest now as it rubbed against the concrete. If the Dry Man hadn't been covered in jail food the guard might have seen that he wasn't simply throwing a tantrum, but was in fact shedding strips of dry skin that in some places exposed brittle bones under paper thin, desiccated muscles. If the guard hadn't been so casually brutal by nature, he might have noticed that his prisoner was actually in serious trouble. But the cell was such a mess and the guard was so inattentive that these warning signs went unheeded. After repeated instructions to hand over the food tray, interspersed with threats of violence, the Dry Man, in a Herculean feat of strength driven by fear managed to pick up the tray with one depleted hand and was just barely able to pass it through the food slot. As the tray was yanked from his withered grasp, the Dry Man managed to whisper with the last of his parched voice, "Please… Cocoa butter. Please…"

The guard gave him a quizzical look, noticing for the first time that beneath the smeared food, this inmate wasn't looking too good. At that point anyone could have seen that the Dry Man was in serious trouble and needed immediate medical attention, but this particular guard was a long standing veteran in the Sheriff's Department and had seen enough death, depravity and violence on the job to no longer care about prisoner welfare. "Not looking too good Buddy. Looks like you're withdrawing pretty hard from the booze. I guess I better get you to the nurse before you go and die on me. Not that I care one way or the other, but if you do croak it will mean a lot of paperwork."

With that, the food slot was slammed shut and the guard made his way down the hall, collecting more empty trays as he went. When he had reached the far end of the long cellblock, he rolled the food cart out of the way for the trustee to take back to the kitchen and got ready for the relaxing portion of his shift. Earlier, he had withheld two meal trays as punishment from some unruly prisoners in the back of the wing. This withholding of food was one of his pet tricks for dealing with troublesome inmates and he often ate the meals in front of the hungry prisoners as further torture. Today, however, his feet were tired so he sat down at his desk, slopping up the disgusting jail food, which he had come to love over the years. He cleaned the food off both trays, drank several cups of coffee, put his feet up on his desk and then promptly fell asleep, snoring lightly while dreaming about his fat wife's chubby sister and all the things he'd love to do to her.

A couple hours later, the next shift arrived waking him from a deeper slumber than he had intended. He had just enough time to wipe the crust from his eyes and regain his feet before the relief guards entered the cellblock to prepare for the shift change. Following procedure, he briefed the officers as to the new intake and filled them in on the details of his rather uneventful night shift. "There's a real cuckoo clock in cell Five B, a drunk admitted last night for killing a pedestrian. I gave him his food tray this morning and when I went to collect it he was wearing his breakfast. Keeps begging for hand lotion or something. You might want to call the nurse and have her take a look at him. Last I checked he wasn't doing too good."

The relief guards registered this information without comment. They too were veterans of the county jail, and over time, had become almost completely uninterested in the plight of their prisoners. They began their bed checks at the first cells by their desk and made their way down the long corridor of the cellblock, one officer on the left side of the corridor and the other officer on the right. This section of the jail was known as D Wing. It was reserved for single cell admitting, protective custody and solitary confinement. Each cell housed one inmate behind a thick steel door. As they made checkmarks after each prisoner's name on a clipboard, they slowly made their way down the hallway, confirming the prisoners were in their cells and still breathing. Midway through their bed check they came to the Dry Man's cell. The guard checking the left side of the hall suddenly called his partner over, "Take a look in this cell." The other officer crossed the hall and his partner leaned aside to let him see through the window.

The guard peered into cell Five B with a puzzled look on his face. Inside, on the concrete floor, was a discarded orange jumpsuit lying next to a pile of gray dust. The observation window offered a complete view of the small cell, but no prisoner could be seen. "Go sound the alarm and get the Warden on the radio. Looks like we have an escape."

As the first officer took off running down the hall towards the panic alarm, the second guard removed a key from the clip on his belt and unlocked the holding cell door. Entering the tiny chamber, he left footprints on the dusty floor as his movements kicked up clouds of fine gray ash into the air. Scanning the entire cell, looking for a place where the prisoner might be hiding, his mind raced to understand where the prisoner had gone. Not finding any satisfactory explanation as to where the inmate could be, the officer turned his attention to the pile of dust on the floor, crouching down for a better look.

Focusing in closer on the dust, the guard began to make

out strange shapes that looked like they had been pressed into the mound. It seemed in places as if the dust pile had been somehow molded to resemble human bones. The guard could make out the shape of a femur pressed out of either fine sand or possibly fireplace ashes. As he crouched there pondering the strange dust, the shape of a skull became apparent at the crest of the mound.

Shifting his weight, and getting down on his hands and knees, the officer moved nearer to the delicate skull shape, wondering how the missing prisoner could have crafted something so fragile and detailed out of a pile of ash. He was so taken in by the mystery of what he was looking at that he didn't even notice the slight tickle in his nose caused by the dust he had inadvertently kicked up into the air. He leaned in really close, peering into the hollow eye sockets of the skull. Before he knew what was happening, without time to stop himself, a mighty sneeze burst forth from his nose effectively eradicating what little remained of the Dry Man.

One Hallway in the Maze

"I've been here for almost two years and I still get lost. The demons behind the locked doors howl night and day. I am sick when it gets cold and suffer from the heat. Everyone here is sick even the doctors and nurses. There is an orderly who corners me whenever he gets the chance. I don't like the way he stares at my body. Trapped in a maze of madness. Diseased in the head. I wish I was dead."

—from a moldy notebook found in the basement of Reception

She's a Ghost

"We were supposed to transport a female patient to another wing and we had her locked up in a restraint chair. We actually had to fight this girl and hit her a few good ones before she could be strapped down. When we were wheeling her away, my partner and I looked back and saw a dark female figure standing in the doorway of the cell. I only caught a brief glimpse because the figure suddenly backed out of view and was gone. When we went to check, the cell was empty and there was nowhere to hide. After the inmate was moved to a new cell we had no further problems so it might have been the ghost tormenting her in there."

—from an email exchange with a former staff member

Sanatorium Days
Overbrook Nights

Journalists and students occasionally ask me about my adventures. The following Q&A is for a Wesleyan University student writing a paper about urban wilderness. His research led him to the Essex Mountain Sanatorium (TB Hospital) and the Essex County Hospital Center (Mental Institution) where I spent so much time playing as a kid. The interview provides some perspective on my own personal experience at the Old Asylum. —wheeler

Where did the legends about the Essex Mountain Sanatorium come from? Did more start circulating after *Weird NJ* began writing about the area?

I had never even heard of the sanatorium, but I stumbled upon it one day while playing in the woods with some friends. We were building forts behind the Fox Hollow housing development in North Caldwell, which was still under construction at the time. The closer we got to the top of the hill, the more junk we began to find. Eventually our quest for building materials led us to a crumbling road which had been used as an illegal dumping ground for many years. After we got bored picking through the trash, we made our way up to the water towers where we first spotted the abandoned buildings looming over the trees. This was around 1987 when the entire hospital was still standing. The dilapidated structures were intimidating to say the least, but they were also darkly inviting. We spent the first few months daring each other to cross the threshold and it was terrifying, but eventually after many repeated visits I began to feel at home inside the sanatorium.

Finding the abandoned hospital when I was ten afforded me about seven years of hanging out in the main buildings before they were torn down. After the county razed the hospital only a few of the outbuildings remained. This was a devastating blow, but the unique geography of the Hilltop prevailed as an impenetrable island of woods in a sea of suburbia. The remaining sanatorium structures continued to be a safe haven for anarchy long after the glory of the main buildings had passed. My friends and I took full advantage of them while they were still around. My early adult years were spent wandering the nurses' quarters, roaming through the forest, and hanging out on the roof of the red brick boiler room. It was during this period that I began consolidating my pictures and putting together the website *welcometohell*. As a means of advertising, I spray painted the web address all over the walls and it didn't take long for the link to get shared across the Internet. After that, there was a noticeable influx of out-of-town visitors to the sanatorium and the legends continued to spread. *Weird NJ* probably contributed to this as well, but unlike my site, *WNJ* has strict rules about not publishing directions to illegal locations. *welcometohell* had maps and tips for not getting caught so I would guess that a lot of people consulted my site before taking the trip.

Can you describe a few of those legends?

The legends were about an abandoned hospital on the top of the hill. For once, the legends were correct!

In your opinion, has *Weird NJ*'s publication of these stories led to a lot more people from out of town showing up at the Hilltop and Overbrook?

Yes, I think that people have become curious about the sanatorium and neighboring Overbrook hospital from what they have read online and in the pages of the magazine. These stories, however, always include the disclaimer that it is illegal to trespass. People who take it upon themselves to enter abandoned buildings can't hold *Weird NJ* or anyone else responsible for the actions they choose to take. It's not illegal to write a story about an abandoned building, but it is illegal to trespass in one.

Did you ever go into the tunnels?

Beneath the sanatorium were tunnels connecting the buildings, which my friends and I thoroughly explored. These underground passages were lined with miles of steam pipes. They were pitch dark, scary as hell, and covered with cave crickets. After the TB hospital was torn down there were only two tunnels left on top of the hill. The first one went from the nurses' building to the boiler room. The second tunnel originated in the boiler room and terminated abruptly in the field where the Administration Building once stood. This tunnel was purposefully collapsed during demolition and marked by a hole in the field. My friend Mad Mike and I spent many hours in this concrete burrow, attempting to clear a passage through the obstruction and gain access to the rest of the tunnels. Unfortunately, the demolition company blocked it with too much rubble and we weren't able to bust through with hand tools. The sanatorium buildings that survived the first round of demolition were finally razed in 2002, but there are ways of getting into the remaining tunnels if you know where to look. (See: *Weird NJ* issue #36 *Hollow Hilltop*)

Further down the hill, at the Essex County Hospital Center, known to locals as Overbrook, there still exists a labyrinth of tunnels beneath the decaying mental hospital. Now that the Old Asylum is closed, the tunnels are black and the entrances are heavily patrolled. You have to be stealthy if you don't want to get caught. This means that flashlights are a bad idea because they attract unwanted attention. Smashing windows and other acts of wanton destruction are totally out of the question. When I was a kid, Overbrook was only partially abandoned. We used to sneak into the tunnels from the hilltop side of Fairview Ave, cross under the street, and watch the patients through the windows of the steel doors. It was always kind of scary looking into the bowels of the working insane asylum and seeing the crazies wandering the basement hallways.

Have you gone to the Hilltop since you were a teenager? If so, how do feel about the new houses? Did you ever go in the jail?

Whenever I drive through that area I try to avoid Mountain Avenue. I can't stand to look at what they've done to my childhood stomping grounds. A few months ago my curiosity got the best of me and I drove up there to see the damage. I was thoroughly sickened by the Mc-Mansions erected on what I consider to be sacred ground, but it does no good to cry about old buildings that have been torn down. All manmade structures will eventually fall. That is their natural and inevitable fate. One day even the McMansions will be abandoned for a future generation of weirdos to enjoy. As for the jail, nah I don't like jails, abandoned or otherwise. I do my best to stay out of prison whenever possible.

Many of the stories I've heard about the Hilltop involve the Sanatorium, and not the nearby Overbrook hospital in Cedar Grove. If that's the case, why are there fewer stories attached to Overbrook?

Actually there are a lot of stories coming out of Overbrook lately. One of the weirdest is about a haunted CPR dummy that is said to wander the halls at night.

Keep in mind, the Essex Mountain Sanatorium was a tuberculosis hospital built in 1901 and abandoned in the 1970s. It wasn't completely demolished until 2002. For three decades the sanatorium stood abandoned on the top of a forested mountain. It was a right of passage for kids growing up in the area to visit the abandoned hospital and scare themselves silly along the way. Stories were passed down through the grades at school and every fall, around Halloween, hordes of teenagers would "discover" the sanatorium for themselves. The isolation that the sanatorium attained high atop Second Mountain made it a one of a kind, never to be repeated paradise in North Jersey.

Meanwhile, during the thirty years that the TB hospital stood abandoned, Overbrook was still very much in operation, treating mental patients and operating a rehab called Turning Point. Many of the outbuildings on the asylum property were neglected and vacant, but most of the main wards were still in use. When it was finally decommissioned and abandoned in 2007, Overbrook held a similar lure for adventure seekers, but the geography surround ing the insane asylum was not as conducive to trespassing as the TB hospital once was.

Overbrook is a sprawling complex on a busy road, making trespassers easy prey for the ever-watchful police. The sanatorium, on the other hand, was an island unto itself where you could smash everything in sight without fear. The theory was that once you got into the building, there wasn't a chance in hell that the police could catch you. This may have been a naïve theory, but I wouldn't know because I never once had to run from the cops. During the fifteen years I spent hanging out on the Hilltop I never got in trouble or heard of anyone being chased by the police. The sanatorium was a forgotten place where parental rules and government laws didn't seem to apply. There were "No Trespassing" signs everywhere, but enforcing them didn't seem to be much of a priority.

In the early years of my sanatorium experience, there was a police van that would occasionally patrol what was left of the paved roads surrounding the complex. The van would make its rounds, sometimes on a 12-hour shift, but since it was the only vehicle up there you could hear it from a mile away. The only time I ever saw the cop get out was to take a leak on the side of the road. This van would appear at random times over the years, but never seemed to deter anybody. I suspect that it was some kind of administrative punishment for an officer to be put on sanatorium duty. It truly was a boring and pointless job, not to mention a complete waste of taxpayer money. The same may hold true for the police driving around Overbrook today because I'm sure when they signed up to be cops it wasn't with the intention of playing babysitter to a bunch of abandoned buildings.

What are some of the stories that stick out most in your mind from the Sanatorium?

I remember sitting in the copper lined gutter of the main hospital, five stories above the courtyard, with my legs dangling in space. I was probably twelve or thirteen years old. In my hand was one of those really big bottles of Southern Comfort. The bottle was half full when I stole it from my friend's parents and I kept it stashed at the sanatorium for a few weeks as I nipped away at it. There I was, five stories above the pavement, swigging the last of the SoCo and feeling no pain. Below me were four teenagers who I didn't know, messing around in the courtyard. Eventually they caught sight of me up on my perch and tried to start a friendly conversation from below. To this day I don't know what the hell I was thinking, but I tipped the whiskey all the way back, swallowed the last gulp of burning fire and launched the oversized bottle into the abyss. It plummeted right at the group of kids and I watched with horror as it fell. This act was so wholly unexpected that the kids just stood there as the bottle came hurtling towards them.

Not only was it a surprise to them, but it also shocked the hell out of me. In my head I had no intention of doing anything like this. It was one of those incredibly stupid and impulsive actions, which seemed to define my adolescence. The bottle exploded on the courtyard pavement within a few feet of the kids. All of them were sprayed with flying glass and they screamed curses at me as they retreated towards Verona where they had probably come from. Despite my considerable buzz, a cold wave of fear ran up my back when I thought about what would have happened had that bottle hit one of those kids. Committing manslaughter was not something I wanted to do, but it was something

SANATORIUM DAYS OVERBROOK NIGHTS

that I had come very close to achieving. This was how I learned not to throw things at people.

One of my weirder stories from the sanatorium happened around the same time period. It is the only shred of evidence I have personally witnessed suggesting ghosts may possibly exist. I have been a skeptic since I was a kid, which is one of the reasons why I was able to get over my fear of the sanatorium as quickly as I did. Those dark hallways were no place for someone who believed in ghosts. Thousands of people died within those wards and even if that hadn't been the case, the place just downright looked haunted. One day my friend Scott and I were patrolling the hallways of the main hospital. We were just leaving the chapel after retrieving my BB gun from the stash place in the ceiling of the auditorium. We walked out into the main hallway when suddenly we heard running boots at the other end of the corridor. Scott was one of the toughest guys I ever met and I had what looked like an authentic machine gun in my hand. We glanced at each other and instinctively took off in pursuit.

The footsteps were booking fast down the hallway towards a bridge that spanned the courtyard's driveway. Because of the way the bridge was situated, there was a slight angle in the hallway that obstructed our view. We couldn't see the person we were running after, but we could hear the fleeing footsteps pounding ahead of our own. As we made the slight turn onto the bridge, we caught a glimpse of our victim as he turned into the hallway of the main building. We heard him run for a few feet, open a door, and slam it behind him. This altercation had taken no more than fifteen seconds from the time we heard him start running to the time he shut the door. We were at the door in an instant and Scott violently kicked it in as I rushed in wielding the BB gun.

The room, as it turned out, was a public bathroom. We kicked in every stall and peered behind every nook and cranny, but there was simply no one there. We checked the ceiling, behind the door, behind the toilets. We looked out the window, which was a 3-story drop onto the asphalt driveway below. We left the bathroom and checked all the rooms in the wing, but there was nobody there. The two of us had left footprints in the plaster dust of the floor, but ours were the only fresh prints to be found. After a while of fruitless searching, we started to get really spooked. I stashed my BB gun back in its hiding place and got the hell out of there. It was a week or more before I was able to shrug it off and return to the sanatorium.

Final Hallway of the Old Asylum

"The mental hospital is coming down fast. Hallways I walked just yesterday are now open-air piles of rubble. The wards that harbored the spirits of insanity for more than a century are now ghosts themselves. I have no regrets about missed opportunities. I took full advantage of the abandoned hospital while it stood. The sanitarium shaped the man I have become and marked itself as an indelible piece of my personal history. The Old Asylum may be gone forever, but I never left the shadow of the buildings."

—from the author's private notebook

Wheeler Antabanez is the author of *gasstationthoughts* (Barricade Books 2001), which caused a stir when he was arrested for its contents. Wheeler is probably best known for his Weird NJ special issue, *Nightshade on the Passaic*, which chronicles his canoe explorations of the Passaic River in New Jersey. He has a forthcoming novel, *Matt and Jess Forever*, and is currently finishing work on his non-fiction speedboat-adventure, *Wheeler on the Passaic*. In addition to writing, Wheeler is renovating a house from the 1800's with his wife, Sara. He has a daughter, Star Magick, of whom he is very proud. Pets include two dogs, three house cats, two outside feral cats, and a tarantula. Antabanez is a lifelong New Jersey resident.

Author photo: Frank Verrone

For more about Wheeler, visit luckycigarette.com.

A Note on the Paintings

The paintings in this book are part of a series called *The Old Asylum: Acrylic on Canvas.* Wheeler executed these original works with black and white acrylic paint on 8×10 canvas boards. The images are direct scans from the paintings and illustrate what the Old Asylum looks like from the author's perspective. The captions accompanying the paintings are fictional in nature, but convey the true essence of the Old Asylum.